## "Is everything

Elliot jumped, his ███████████████████████ d
that Polly was ben████████████████████████
window. Before he ██████████████████████ und
himself taking rapid stock of large hazel eyes, a
straight little nose, perfectly curved Cupid's-bow
lips, and his racing heart raced a bit faster. He hadn't
noticed it before, but all of a sudden he realized how
attractive she was…

"Are you sure you're okay?"

A slim hand closed around his arm and Elliot
flinched. It wasn't her touch per se but the effect it
had on him. Heat poured through his veins so that all
of a sudden it felt as though he was on fire. What the
hell was going on? Why was he burning up because
this woman had touched him? It certainly fell beyond
the range of rational explanation. All he could do
was pray it would stop, and soon. Before the damage
became permanent.

Panic rose inside him, adding to the conflagration.
He didn't want to respond to her this way, didn't
want to start yearning for things he had sworn he
didn't need. He wanted his life to remain exactly the
same as it had been for the past eight years, and yet
he had a feeling that it was already too late, that what
had happened today had changed things, changed
*him*. He took a deep breath as his vision swam. Today
was going to affect his whole future, and there wasn't
a thing he could do about it!

Dear Reader,

I love writing a series of books as it gives me the chance to revisit some favorite characters as well as create new ones. I couldn't wait to start the second book in The Larches Practice series because I had two wonderful new characters in mind.

Community midwife Polly Davies loves her job, and the moms who come under her care love her, as well. She is kind and caring, and she definitely doesn't deserve to be jilted on her wedding day! When she meets pediatric surgeon Elliot Grey, she finds him cold and aloof. She doesn't take to him at all until she realizes that he has a softer side he deliberately chooses to keep hidden.

Elliot was deeply hurt by the breakup of his marriage and has never really gotten over it. He has devoted his life since then to his work and caring for his son, Joseph, who has a disability. Although Polly is still reeling from the shock of her wedding being called off, she finds herself drawn to this enigmatic man. Can she make him see that he is wrong to push people away and that he deserves to be happy?

Bringing Polly and Elliot together was a challenge. Elliot was determined to guard his emotions even from me! I hope you enjoy their story and feel as I do that they deserve their happy ending.

Love,

*Jennifer*

# BRIDE FOR THE
# SINGLE DAD

———

## JENNIFER TAYLOR

**HARLEQUIN**® MEDICAL ROMANCE™

Recycling programs for this product may not exist in your area.

ISBN-13: 978-0-373-21555-3

Bride for the Single Dad

First North American Publication 2017

Copyright © 2017 by Jennifer Taylor

Printed in U.S.A.

www.Harlequin.com

**Books by Jennifer Taylor**

**Harlequin Medical Romance**

*The Larches Practice*
*The Boss Who Stole Her Heart*

*Saving His Little Miracle*
*One More Night with Her Desert Prince…*
*Best Friend to Perfect Bride*
*Miracle Under the Mistletoe*
*The Greek Doctor's Secret Son*
*Reawakened by the Surgeon's Touch*

Visit the Author Profile page
at Harlequin.com for more titles.

# CHAPTER ONE

WHY DID THIS have to happen today of all days? Surely she had enough to contend with, without this as well!

Polly Davies struggled to contain her frustration as she brought her car to a halt. Opening the door, she hurried over to where two vehicles had collided in the centre of the carriageway. It was barely six a.m. and there was no other traffic about but Polly was very aware that if the accident had happened later then it could have been a different story. A lot of people could have been injured then so it seemed that even the darkest cloud could have a silver lining. Maybe that maxim could be applied to her own situation?

Polly bit back a sob, knowing that now wasn't the time to dwell on what had happened. Right now her main concern was to check if anyone had been injured. It appeared that one of the vehicles had run into the back of the other. It was a very expensive car too, the logo on its bonnet declaring its pedigree for all the world to admire. Even as she watched, a tall dark-haired man climbed out of the driver's seat, cursing under his breath when he saw the dent in the front bumper. It was obvious that he wasn't seriously injured, however, so Polly headed towards the other vehicle, her footsteps quickening when she recognised it as the van belonging to the Applethwaite family. They used it to deliver their famous Dales lamb to the local shops and restaurants, but it was only as she drew closer that she realised Lauren Applethwaite was driving it. Polly's heart sank. At three months pregnant, and with a history of miscarriages, this was the last thing that poor Lauren needed.

'Lauren, are you all right?' Polly demanded, opening the van door.

'I don't know. I had this terrible pain...' Lauren broke off and groaned. 'There it is again!'

'Just try to stay calm,' Polly instructed when she heard the panic in Lauren's voice. She leant into the van, knowing that she couldn't risk moving Lauren until she was sure that she hadn't suffered a spinal injury. Her heart sank that bit more because the last thing she wanted was for Lauren to become even more upset if she had to remain in the van. The calmer she was, the better it would be for her baby...

'Stop! For heaven's sake, woman, have you no sense?'

Polly stopped dead when she heard a deep voice behind her. Turning, she saw the driver of the other vehicle striding towards her. He glared down at her and she shivered when she saw the hostility in his green eyes. As the community midwife, she was used to dealing with all types of people. However, she had never seen such naked animosity on anyone's face before.

'You never, *ever*, move an accident victim until you're sure they haven't suffered a spinal injury,' he rapped out.

Polly flushed, resenting both his tone and his assumption that she had no idea what she was doing. However, before she could explain that she had been about to check that it was safe to move Lauren, he elbowed her aside. Sliding his hand between Lauren's back and the seat, he gently ran his fingers down her spine, and Polly frowned. There was a confidence about his actions that pointed towards the fact that he knew exactly what he was doing. It was on the tip of her tongue to ask him if he was medically trained when he turned to her and the question froze on her lips when once again she was treated to an openly hostile look. It made her wonder if he had a problem with her in particular or with women in general before she dismissed the thought. She had enough problems of her own without worrying about his.

The thought of what had happened in the past few hours rose up and swamped her before she could stop it. She should have realised that something was terribly wrong when Martin had failed to phone her last night, she thought, feeling the bitter tears stinging her eyes. She had tried calling him but she had been put straight through to voicemail. She must have left a dozen messages, asking him to phone her back, but when he still hadn't replied by midnight she had got into her car and driven to the cottage they had bought. Martin's parents had given them the deposit as a wedding present and Polly had been thrilled

at the thought of them starting their married
life in their very own home.

It had been a relief to find lights on when
she had reached the cottage. At least it appeared that Martin hadn't had an accident
even if he hadn't returned her calls, Polly had
thought as she had let herself in. However, her
anxiety had soon started to rise again as she
had checked each room and found no sign of
him. It was only when she had gone back to
the sitting room that she had seen the enve-
lope propped up on the mantelpiece...

'There doesn't appear to be anything
wrong with her spine from what I can tell,
but it would be better if we wait until the ambulance gets here before we attempt to move
her.'

Polly dragged her thoughts back to the
current situation when the man spoke to her.
'That won't be possible,' she said, blanking
out the thought of the furore it was going
to cause when everyone found out what had
happened. She forced down the fresh wave of
panic that hit her, aware that there was nothing she could do about it. 'We need to get her
out of there immediately.'

'There's no way that I'm prepared to take

that risk,' he countered, his dark brows drawing together into a frown. It was obvious that he didn't appreciate her arguing with him but Polly wasn't going to let that deter her. Stepping away from the van, she beckoned for him to join her.

'Lauren is three months pregnant,' she explained flatly. 'She has a history of miscarriages and has just told me that she's having pains. She needs to lie down if we're to have any chance at all of saving this baby.'

'And you're an expert on these matters, are you?'

'Yes, as it happens I am.' Polly bridled at the disparaging note in his voice. Normally, she would have let it pass but not today when she was already feeling so emotional. She looked coldly back at him. 'I'm the community midwife for this area and Lauren is one of my patients. I think I can safely say that I know what I'm talking about.'

Elliot Grey could feel his temper soaring, which was unusual for him but he really didn't need this aggravation on top of everything else that had happened recently. He had spent the past week trying to sort out the mess he had found himself in and he had failed. Miserably. He was no closer to finding anyone reliable to look after his son, Joseph, than he'd been this time last week. Not for the first time, he found himself wondering if he had made a huge mistake by moving to the Yorkshire Dales. Back in London, he could have contacted any of a dozen agencies and there would have been a highly qualified nanny knocking on his door a couple of hours later. Granted, he would have had to pay through the nose for such a service but money didn't matter: making sure Joseph was safe and happy was his only concern...

But Joseph hadn't been happy, had he? Elliot thought suddenly. Joseph had hated the constant changes, the fact that no sooner had a new nanny been hired then she would find another job and leave. That was why Elliot had decided to leave the city and relocate to the country. It would be easier to find someone permanent to care for Joseph while he was at work in a place where there were fewer jobs available, he had reasoned. However, it certainly hadn't worked out that way. The woman he had hired had backed out at the last moment and finding anyone else quali-

fied to look after an eight-year-old with major
health issues was proving an uphill battle...

'*Hello?* I hate to rush you but I would like
to get this sorted out this side of Christmas
if it isn't too much trouble.'

The sarcasm in the woman's voice roused
him. Elliot glowered at the tall, red-haired
woman who was watching him with what
looked very much like disdain on her face. It
was a whole new experience to have anyone
look at him that way too. None of his former
colleagues would have dared and, as for anyone else, then he would have soon put them
in their place. However, he had a feeling that
this woman cared little about upsetting him
and it made him feel strangely vulnerable to
realise that his disapproval meant nothing to
her.

Elliot dismissed that thought as the fanciful
nonsense it undoubtedly was. Moving back
to the van, he peered inside, his reservations
about moving the driver disappearing when
he saw the pain on her face. It was obvious
that they needed to get her out of there as
quickly as possible.

'I've a rug in my car—I'll go and fetch it.'
He glanced round when the red-haired

woman spoke beside him, feeling his senses swirl as he inhaled the fragrance of the shampoo she had used to wash her hair. It was years since he had been aware of something like that and it shook him so that he missed what she said next. 'I'm sorry—what was that?' he asked thickly.

'Can you phone for an ambulance while I fetch the rug?' she repeated. 'Lauren's in a great deal of pain and she needs to be in hospital.'

Elliot nodded, not trusting himself to say anything this time, although it was understandable if he was acting out of character after the week he'd had. The thought helped to reassure him as he took his mobile phone from his pocket and put through a call to the emergency services. He sighed inwardly when the operator explained that it would take some time for the ambulance to reach them. The sooner this was over and done with, the sooner he could get home to Joseph, he thought anxiously as he ended the call. Asking Mrs Danton, his newly acquired housekeeper, to spend the night with his son had been a last resort, but he'd had no choice when he had been called into work. However, he couldn't expect Mrs Danton to keep covering for him so he would need to find someone suitable to look after Joseph soon… *if he could.*

The thought of what little success he'd had to date didn't sit easily with him. It was a relief when the red-haired woman came back and he could turn his attention to other matters. Elliot moved aside while she bent down to speak to the driver.

'We're going to get you out of there now, Lauren. We'll take it nice and slowly so there's nothing to worry about. The ambulance is on its way and it won't be long before it gets here.'

Elliot felt a ripple of something that felt very much like shame run through him and he frowned. Why did he feel ashamed to hear genuine concern in her voice? Was it the fact that he was more concerned about his own problems than this poor woman? When was the last time he had really felt anything? he wondered suddenly. When had he truly cared? Oh, he cared about Joseph, of course, cared about every aspect of his son's life. It was his *raison d'être,* the thing that kept him focused. He also cared about utilising his skills to give his young patients a better quality of life, but even then his interest was detached, impersonal. He didn't feel it inside, didn't feel anything very much in there. Apart from his love for Joseph, his heart was a wasteland, empty, barren, and all of a sudden Elliot found himself wishing that it was different, that *he* was different. Listening to this woman, with her concern and her caring, he realised how much he was lacking.

'Can you swing your legs out, Lauren? I know it hurts, love, but we need to lie you down.'

The woman's voice was gentle, soothing, and for some reason Elliot felt his guilt subside. Moving closer to the van, he waited until the driver had swung her legs out of the door. 'I'll carry her,' he said gruffly because old habits took a long time to die.

'Are you sure you can manage?'

The redhead shot an assessing look at him, obviously weighing up his physique, and Elliot felt himself colour. It happened so fast too that he didn't have time to stop it. Bending, he gathered the driver into his arms, feeling heat scudding around his body. He couldn't recall ever blushing like this before, would swear that he had never done so, not even when he was a teenager, and the shock of what had happened robbed him of the ability to speak. He could only nod like some damned puppet as he carried the young woman over to the pavement and gently laid her down on the rug.

'Thank you.' The red-haired woman stepped around him and knelt down. 'Where exactly is the pain, Lauren? Can you show me?'

'Here.' Lauren pointed to the lower right-hand side of her abdomen and Elliot frowned.

'Appendix?' he murmured, not realising that he had spoken out loud until the redhead looked sharply at him.

'Was that a lucky guess or do you have some kind of medical training?'

'Medical training,' he said shortly. He had a list of qualifications as long as his arm but he wasn't about to share them with her and have her make some disparaging remark. It shook him that he should be so sensitive all of a sudden and he hurried on. 'I'll check with ambulance control to see how long it will be before they get here.'

'You do that. And, while you're speaking

to them, make sure they know the patient is three months pregnant with a history of miscarriages.' Her tone was laced with genuine concern once more. 'They need to be prepared when we get there.'

Elliot didn't say anything as he moved away to make the call but it didn't stop him thinking it. Somewhere along the line he had forgotten why he had gone into medicine in the first place—to alleviate suffering and help people. Would he ever find his way back to those days when he had cared? he wondered. Return to a time when each and every patient he had treated had left their mark? He hoped so, he really did. Because he knew with a sudden flash of insight that he would never be truly happy unless he did.

It was almost eight a.m. before Polly felt that she could safely leave the hospital. Lauren had been rushed to Theatre as it appeared that her appendix was on the point of rupturing. A scan had shown that her baby was safe and well and now she just needed to get through the operation. Although it wasn't ideal in her condition, the surgeon seemed confident that all would be well.

'Thanks again for everything you've done, Polly.' Lauren's husband, Sam, hugged her. 'Having you there really helped Lauren—it stopped her panicking so much.'

'I was happy to help, and even happier that the surgeon is so positive about the outcome.' She hugged Sam back. 'Everything will be fine, Sam, you'll see.'

'I hope so.' Sam dredged up a smile, but it was obvious that he was deeply worried about them losing this much-wanted child. 'Anyway, you get off now. Lauren will never forgive herself if you're late because of her.'

'Tell her from me that she's not to give it another thought,' Polly said quickly. She bit her lip, wondering if she should explain, but her brother, Peter, had insisted that he would be the one to break the news. She had phoned him as soon as she had read the letter Martin had left for her. Peter was based in New York these days and had only flown into the country that afternoon but he had hired a car and driven straight over to Beesdale. They had spent the night discussing what to do until in the end Peter had insisted that she should leave it to him. It had been a relief, if she was honest. The thought of the upset it was going to cause so many people wasn't something she relished, so she would do as Peter had suggested, drive to York and catch the train to London as she and Martin had planned to do. At least it would give her a breathing space, time to make fresh plans, because that was what she was going to have to do now, of course.

It was a scary thought. Polly did her best not to panic as she said goodbye and left. She would take things one step at a time and eventually she would come out the other side, even though she couldn't imagine what her life was going to be like in the future. A sob caught in her throat. All her plans were up in the air; everything she had expected to happen now wouldn't take place. It was a daunting prospect, to say the least.

Polly was so deep in thought that she had made her way outside before she remembered that she had left her car in Beesdale. Lauren had begged her to go in the ambulance with her and Polly hadn't given any thought to what she would do after she left the hospital. She sighed wearily. If her case hadn't been in the car then she could have taken a taxi to the station but she would need the clothes she had packed, even if they had been chosen for a very different reason…

'Do you want a lift?'

Polly glanced round when a taxi drew up alongside her, her eyebrows rising when she recognised the man seated in the back as the driver of the other vehicle involved in the accident. 'What are you doing here?' she said with a sad lack of grace.

'It appears that I've pulled a muscle.' He winced as he carefully rotated his shoulder. 'The paramedics insisted I should be checked over—something to do with any action my insurance company may decide to take in the future. It's a lot of fuss about nothing, in my opinion.'

'It's always safer to get these things checked out,' Polly murmured, feeling guilty that she hadn't asked him earlier if he had been injured. She had been too busy putting him in his place and it wasn't like her to behave that way but, there again, nothing that had happened in the last eight hours was normal. Once again she felt panic well up inside her. Could she cope with a future that was going to be so very different from the one she had planned?

'Look, do you want a lift or not? You may have nothing to do today but I need to get home.'

The impatience in the man's voice was just what she needed to steady her. Polly glared at him. 'Are you always this charming? Or are you making a special effort just for me?'

'Believe me, I have treated you *exactly* the same as everyone else,' he retorted.

'Then you obviously need to work on your people skills,' Polly shot back, wrenching open the taxi door.

She settled back in the seat as the driver set off, feeling weariness wash over her. The lack of sleep plus all the emotional turmoil she'd been through had left her feeling drained. Opening her bag, she took out the letter that Martin had left for her, forcing herself to re-read the few brief lines it contained. It was still hard to believe it was true but there it was, in black and white. He had met someone else and, although he was very sorry, he had realised that he wanted to be with her and not Polly. In the meantime, he was going away and would leave it to Polly to tell everyone that the wedding was cancelled. If she preferred to say that it had been a mutual decision then that was fine with him. He only hoped that in time she would understand that he had made the right decision for both of them.

Polly took a deep breath as she folded up the letter and put it back in her bag. She hoped so too, hoped that a time would come when she didn't feel so completely and utterly at sea. She glanced at her watch, feeling the ready tears scalding her eyes. In a couple of hours' time everyone in Beesdale would know that she wasn't getting married today.

# CHAPTER TWO

ELLIOT REACHED FOR his wallet as the taxi drew up. He still wasn't sure why he had offered the woman a lift. Normally, it wouldn't have crossed his mind and yet the moment he had seen her standing outside A&E he had felt compelled to help her. Why? Because she had looked so lost, so forlorn? Why should he care how she felt? He had no idea but he could have no more left her standing there than he could have…have flown to the *moon*!

'Here we are then,' he said, dismissing that ridiculous thought as they climbed out of the cab. He drummed up a smile, making an effort to appear a shade more cordial than he had been earlier. Just for a moment he was tempted to explain about the frustrating week he'd had before he thought better of it. Explanations were for the weak, for those people who were prepared to give others an advantage over them. And he had decided many years ago that he would never let anyone take advantage of him again. 'Right back where we started.'

'Oh…erm…yes.'

The woman jumped as though she had been lost in a world of her own and once again Elliot's interest was piqued. Was she worrying about Lauren and her baby, he wondered, or was there something else troubling her? The question hovered on his lips but he forced it back. He wouldn't ask, wouldn't invite any confidences, wouldn't get involved in any way at all. His life was fine the way it was. He had Joseph and his work to fill it and he didn't need anything else. If and when he needed sex then he organised it with the same attention to detail that he arranged everything else. He always chose a woman who felt the same as he did, who didn't want commitment but merely wanted to satisfy a need. He knew without even having to think about it that this woman didn't fall into that category. No, she would expect the lot—marriage, commitment, a lifetime of togetherness—all the things he had sworn he would avoid after he and Marianna had divorced.

The thought of his ex-wife made his mouth tighten and he saw the woman beside him colour. Reaching into her bag, she took out her car keys. 'I won't detain you any longer. Thank you for the lift. I appreciated it.'

With that, she walked over to her car. Elliot watched her go, wondering why he felt as though he should have said something, but what exactly? Should he have thanked her for stopping earlier, perhaps? After all, if the accident had happened in the city then few people would have stopped—they would have been too busy with their own affairs to help a stranger. He would have had to deal with it himself, deal with the other driver as well. Although it wouldn't have been a problem as such; after all, he was medically qualified. But would Lauren have told him that she was pregnant or would she have been put off by his attitude? The thought that she might not have disclosed the information settled like a heavy weight inside him. He couldn't help wondering what other information he had missed over the years because people had been deterred by his less than encouraging approach. What had the redhead said before—that he needed to work on his people skills? It seemed she was right.

Elliot could feel all sorts of emotions swirling around inside him as he headed to his car. It was years since he had felt so unsure about his actions and it shook him. Every aspect of his life, from the tiniest detail to the most major decision, was always planned in advance. To find himself awash with doubts all of a sudden was scary. It made him feel vulnerable, defenceless.

'Is everything all right?'

Elliot jumped, his heart racing, when he discovered that the woman was bending down beside the open window. Before he could stop himself, he found himself taking rapid stock of large hazel eyes, a straight little nose, a perfectly curved Cupid's bow, and his racing heart raced a bit faster. He hadn't noticed it before but all of a sudden he realised how attractive she was...

'Are you sure you're OK?'

A slim hand reached in and closed around his arm and Elliot flinched. It wasn't her touch per se but the effect it had on him. Heat poured through his veins so that all of a sudden it felt as though he was on fire. What the hell was going on? Why was he burning up because this woman had touched him? It certainly fell beyond the range of rational explanation. All he could do was pray it would stop—and stop soon. Stop before the damage became permanent.

Panic rose inside him, adding to the conflagration. He didn't want to respond to her this way, didn't want to start yearning for things he had sworn he didn't need. He wanted his life to remain exactly the same as it had been for the past eight years, and yet he had a feeling that it was already too late, that what had happened today had changed things, changed *him*. He took a deep breath as his vision swam. Today was going to affect his whole future and there wasn't a thing he could do about it either!

Polly could feel the heat of the man's skin flowing through her fingertips and frowned. Although it was a warm day for April, it wasn't so warm that it should have caused such a rise in his temperature. Sliding her hand down to his wrist, she checked his pulse, her frown deepening when she discovered how rapid it was. He'd told her that he had strained a muscle but that didn't explain why his pulse was racing like this, did it?

'Do you feel sick or dizzy?' she said, bending closer so that she could look into his eyes. Maybe he had hit his head when he had run into the back of the van, she thought anxiously. It was a known fact that a head injury could take some time to present itself and if it was left untreated it could have disastrous consequences. The thought sent a rush of fear scudding through her.

'Are you sure you didn't hit your head?' Polly said urgently, checking his pupils for any irregularities, a sure sign of a head injury.

'No. I just wrenched my neck.'

His voice was deep, husky, and Polly felt a frisson run through her. All of a sudden she was aware of him in a way she had never expected to be. She let her gaze travel over his face in the hope that she would find some clue there to explain what was happening. His eyes were green, a deep sea-green, framed by thick black lashes. His eyebrows were black too, making his skin appear paler than she would have expected, apart from along his jaw where the shadow of stubble had darkened it. His features were, frankly, uncompromising, the chiselled lines of his nose and jaw adding to the impression of a man who gave few concessions in life. Only his mouth hinted at a gentler side, the full lower lip looking disturbingly sensual. What would it be like to kiss him? Polly wondered. To feel his mouth on hers, hard and demanding at first, before his lips softened...

Heat flashed through her veins and she drew back abruptly, scared by the feelings that thought had aroused. She couldn't recall feeling this kind of raw desire before, not even when she and Martin had made love. If she was honest, their lovemaking had been a disappointment. Although she'd had a couple of affairs during her time at college, she didn't have a huge amount of experience and she had wondered if that was why their lovemaking hadn't lived up to her expectations. Now she realised that it hadn't been solely her fault and that Martin had been equally to blame. Oh, he might have gone through the motions of making love to her but had his heart been in it when he had met someone else? Someone he had wanted more than her? Polly sighed sadly. A lot of heartache could have been avoided if only Martin had found the courage to tell her the truth. It was a relief when the sound of a mobile phone ringing cut through her unhappy thoughts.

'Elliot Grey.' The man pressed a button on the dashboard and answered the call.

'It's Sister Thomas, sir. I'm afraid little Alfie Nolan's condition has deteriorated. Dr Walters wants to take him to Theatre. He feels the faulty heart valve needs to be replaced immediately.'

Polly bit back a gasp as she listened to the conversation. So this was Elliot Grey! Oh, she'd heard about him, of course: who hadn't? That one of the country's leading paediatric surgeons had chosen to head up the team at their local hospital had set everyone talking. Polly had been as surprised as everyone else that he had opted to leave London and relocate to Yorkshire, and now that she had met him her amazement knew no bounds. Maybe it was naïve to make such an assumption but surely a man who spent his life caring for the most vulnerable patients should be more, well…*approachable*?

'Tell Dr Walters that I shall be there as soon as I can. In the meantime, he's to do nothing.' Elliot Grey cut the connection without further ado. Polly suspected that he considered such niceties as saying goodbye a waste of his time. Scrolling down the list of telephone numbers, he selected one, speaking as soon as the call was answered. 'It's Elliot Grey. I have to go back to the hospital so I shall need you to stay with my son until I get back, Mrs Danton.'

'I'm sorry, Dr Grey, but that isn't possible. I'm looking after my grandchildren this morning while my daughter's at work and I'm already late as it is,' Iris Danton replied firmly.

'Surely your daughter can find someone else to mind them,' Elliot snapped back. 'This is an emergency, after all.'

'Maybe it is, but there'll be another emergency if my daughter loses her job. No, I stepped in last night to help you but I can't do it again today.'

With that the woman hung up. Polly sympathised with her because it was a bit rich to expect her to let down her daughter to fit in with Elliot Grey's plans. However, she also knew how urgent it was that he returned to the hospital and it was that which made her speak up, that and nothing else. It definitely had nothing to do with all those crazy feelings that had swept through her a few minutes earlier.

'I can mind your son if you're stuck.'

'You?' Elliot Grey turned icy green eyes on her and Polly almost took a step back. She forced herself to stand her ground, wondering why he was so hostile when she was offering to do him a favour.

'Yes, me. As I told you, I'm the community midwife for this area, so I think you can trust me to take good care of him.' She shrugged when he just kept on staring at her. 'My name's Polly Davies. You can call the maternity unit if you want to check I'm who I say I am. They'll vouch for me.'

'I don't doubt you are who you claim to be, Miss Davies. However, I do wonder why you would offer to look after Joseph. Out of the goodness of your heart, perhaps, or because you have an ulterior motive?'

'An ulterior motive?' Polly repeated blankly.

'Yes. Now that you know who I am, I can't help but wonder if you're looking to earn yourself some Brownie points.' His tone was clipped and Polly felt that shiver run through her again, the one she'd felt earlier when they had first met. It took her all her time not to let him see how much it disturbed her.

'I've no idea what you mean.'

'No? I thought my views on community midwives were widely known but apparently not. So, to reiterate, I am totally opposed to women having their babies at home, which is the approach you favour. In my opinion every baby should be born in the safety of a fully equipped maternity unit so that any problems can be dealt with promptly. To be blunt, Miss Davies, I would ban you and the rest of your cohorts from delivering any more babies if I could!'

Elliot knew that it had been tactless in the extreme to have said that but he couldn't stop himself. He had seen far too many damaged children to change his views. Every child should be born in hospital and allowing home births to take place in this day and age was a disgrace, in his opinion. He would have dearly loved to expound his views but a glance at the dashboard clock put paid to that. He needed to get back to the hospital, but how could he when there was nobody to look after Joseph…? Unless he took Polly Davies up on her offer, always assuming she was still willing after him shooting her down like that.

'I had no idea you held such stringent views, Dr Grey. Obviously, they haven't filtered through to me. However, much as I would love to debate the points you raised, I doubt if this is the right time. My offer still stands and, no, I don't expect any Brownie points for looking after your son. I'm not that naïve.'

'Thank you.' Elliot gritted his teeth, desperately trying to hold back the apology that hovered on the tip of his tongue. That he should feel the need to apologise when he knew he was right was shock enough; however, the fact that he was so desperate to make amends was an even bigger one. What was it about this woman that made him feel so out of control? he wondered as he started the car. She had the ability to make him doubt himself and he didn't enjoy the experience. He liked to be fully in control of himself— no, not liked, *needed*. It made him feel safe.

Elliot drove that disturbing thought from his head, not wanting her to suspect how on edge he felt. 'I suggest you follow me home so I can introduce you to Joseph. I've bought the old blacksmith's cottage in Trefoil Lane—do you know it?'

'Yes,' she replied succinctly then turned away. Going over to her car, she started the engine, not waiting for him as she set off.

Elliot slid the powerful car into gear, curbing the urge to put his foot down and overtake her when they reached the open road. So she didn't need him to lead the way—so what? If she was trying to prove her independence then he didn't care. He didn't care about anyone except Joseph. The strange thing was that, no matter how hard he tried to convince himself, it didn't ring true. Deep down inside, in some long-abandoned place, he did care. He cared a lot, cared about her opinion of him. Foolish though he knew it was, he didn't want Polly Davies to think badly of him.

It was almost nine a.m. when Polly drew up outside The Old Smithy, as the cottage was known locally. She could hear the clock on Beesdale Church chiming the hour as she got out of the car and sighed. By rights she should have been on the train by now, but what else could she have done in the circumstances?

Elliot Grey needed her help even if he had been less than gracious about accepting it. Did he honestly think that she had been trying to worm her way into his good books by offering to mind his son? she thought as she walked up the path. Well, if that were the case, he was in for a shock. He might think he was next to God in the pecking order but he was a long way from being that, in her opinion!

'Come along. I need to get back to the hospital as soon as possible.'

The subject of her thoughts swept past her and opened the front door. Polly's mouth thinned as she followed him inside. Would it hurt him to employ a few basic good manners? she thought sourly. Behave like any normal person would do in the circumstances? She didn't expect him to go over the top—just to appear grateful would be enough. However, it seemed that gratitude and Elliot Grey weren't acquainted with one another.

She followed him along the hall, taking stock as she went. She knew that the cottage had been converted by its previous owners, a couple from London who had used it as a weekend retreat until travelling back and forth had become too much of a hassle. They had spent a fortune on it, if rumour was to be believed, and the original cottage now encompassed what had once been the blacksmith's forge.

However, it wasn't until she stepped into the kitchen that she realised just how much it had changed. The room was enormous and wonderfully spacious despite the impressive range of top-end fitments. Polly sighed as she drank it all in, from the marble-topped island in the centre to the cosy family corner complete with squashy leather sofa. It was the kitchen she and Martin had dreamed about, not that they could have hoped to own a place as spectacular as this even if they had got married...

'Who are you?'

The question brought her back to earth with a bump. Polly turned to find a small boy of about eight years of age watching her with an all too familiar expression in his green eyes. Talk about a chip off the old block, she thought ruefully as she took in the dark brown hair, the clean-cut features, not to mention the air of reserve the child projected. He had to be Elliot's son; the resemblance was too marked for him not to be. The only thing that set him apart from his father was the fact that he was in a wheelchair.

Polly's gaze flew to Elliot and her heart seemed to scrunch up inside her when she saw the expression on his face, all the love mingled with a fear that she might say something to hurt the child. In that moment everything she felt about him was turned on its head, turned upside down and inside out as well. Now he was no longer a pain in the proverbial, some insufferable, self-opinionated man who needed putting in his place. Now he was simply a loving father who wanted to protect his child, and Polly realised that she could forgive him anything because of that.

# CHAPTER THREE

'MY NAME'S POLLY DAVIES. And you must be Joseph. How do you do?'

Elliot let out the breath he hadn't even known he was holding as Polly reached out and shook Joseph's hand. She didn't do what so many folk did, what they thought they *should* do, and bend down so she was on his son's level. She simply held out her hand and that was it, and it was a form of acceptance of Joseph's condition that touched him in ways Elliot could barely understand. Polly wasn't pretending that Joseph was the same as every other child his age, but she wasn't making an issue of it either by overcompensating. He cleared his throat, trying to dislodge the unfamiliar lump that had found its way there.

'Polly is going to look after you while I go back to the hospital, Joseph.'

'Is the baby still not well?' Joseph spun

his wheelchair around, his face alight with interest. Elliot had no idea if it was right or wrong but he always discussed his cases with him. Joseph had become his sounding board, in a way; he ran through what he had done, checking in his own mind that he couldn't have done more, and Joseph listened even if he didn't always understand the complexities of what he was hearing.

'No. Sadly one of his heart valves isn't working properly. It needs replacing so I'll have to go back and see to it. Mrs Danton has to mind her grandchildren this morning so Polly has offered to stay with you.' It was the first time that Elliot had said Polly's name and he felt the tiniest frisson run down his spine, like fairy footsteps tiptoeing over his skin. He wasn't sure why it was happening and certainly wasn't going to make the mistake of searching for an explanation so he hurried on. 'Is that all right with you?'

'Uh-huh.' Joseph shot an assessing glance at Polly. 'Are you a nanny?'

'No. I'm a midwife,' she replied evenly, not at all put out, it appeared, about being cross-questioned.

'So you work at the hospital?' Joseph continued, weighing up what she had said.

'No. I'm a community midwife. I deliver babies at home and also take care of the mums before and after their babies are born.'

'Dad thinks you lot should be banned,' Joseph told her, ignoring Mrs Danton's tut of disapproval. 'He says you do more harm than good.'

'So I believe.' Polly glanced at him and Elliot stiffened in readiness for what would come next. 'Sadly, even the cleverest people can be wrong sometimes, Joseph.'

Joseph laughed, his small face lighting up with amusement. 'Dad won't like you saying that—do you, Dad?'

'Ahem. It's a discussion best left till another time,' Elliot murmured, feeling as though he had been caught flat-footed. He had expected a far more acerbic response and he wasn't sure what to make of it. Surely Polly wasn't softening towards him…was she?

Those wretched fairies were at it again, running fairy-sized raccs up and down his spine, and he had to force himself not to get side-tracked by that strangely appealing thought. Mrs Danton was putting on her coat and he thanked her for minding Joseph then turned to Polly as soon as she had left. 'I don't know how long I'll be so you may need to sort out something for lunch. Joseph can show you where everything is.'

'Fine. It's not a problem.' She shrugged off her coat and tossed it over a chair then went to the kettle and switched it on. 'How about a drink, Joseph? Juice? Milk? Hot chocolate? What do you fancy?'

'Cola,' Joseph replied immediately.

'Oh, no,' Elliot began but he got no further.

'Nice try, sunshine, but I doubt if your dad lets you have fizzy drinks at this time of the day, so choose something else,' Polly said firmly.

'Milk then,' Joseph muttered, rolling his eyes.

'Coming right up.'

She went to the huge American-style refrigerator, took out the milk then opened a cupboard and took out a glass. Elliot watched in amazement, marvelling at how at home she seemed to be. He was still finding his way around, opening cupboard after cupboard before he found what he wanted, and it was galling to admit it, galling too that she had dealt with Joseph so efficiently. People had a tendency to let him get away with things because of his disability, but not Polly. She had treated him the same as she would have treated any other child and, for the first time since Joseph was born, Elliot felt redundant. He wasn't sure if he liked the idea either.

'I'd better get going,' he said gruffly, realising how ridiculous he was being. He should be glad that Joseph seemed happy to let Polly look after him. 'Can you walk me out?'

'Of course.' Polly grinned at the little boy. 'Your dad's probably going to give me a list of dos and don'ts so be warned: I shall be completely up to speed when it comes to any more dodgy requests, young man!'

Joseph laughed again and Elliot hid his amazement because it wasn't like him to take to a stranger so readily. Joseph could be difficult at times yet he seemed to have responded instantly to Polly the same as he, himself, had done. It was another thought that Elliot didn't intend to give any room to. He strode along the hall, only halting when he reached the front door. Polly had stopped as well, so close that once again he could smell the scent of her shampoo, a fragrance that made his senses tingle… *Clang!* The barriers came down, shutting off that idea before it could go any further. He never entertained such fanciful thoughts about any woman and he refused to start now.

'Joseph has medication he needs to take,' he said, enunciating every word as he strove to clear his mind. 'The details of time and dosage is in the top drawer of my desk in the study, along with the tablets he takes.' He pointed out the room. 'Any problems then phone me. My number's on speed dial, along with the number of Joseph's consultant in London. You can phone him if there's a problem and I'm unavailable for any reason.'

'Isn't Joseph registered at The Larches surgery?' Polly asked, frowning.

'He is, but I would prefer it if you contacted his consultant if there's a problem and you can't reach me. Professor Rose has been responsible for Joseph's care since he was a baby and he's fully conversant with his case.'

'I see. What exactly is wrong with Joseph?'

'Spina bifida,' Elliot replied succinctly. He knew it was stupid but he still found it difficult to talk about his son's condition. Guilt rose up inside him, as it did every time he had to explain what was wrong with Joseph. He should have checked that Marianna was following her consultant's advice and taking the supplements he had prescribed then maybe Joseph wouldn't have been born with this condition!

'I imagine it was detected during his mother's pregnancy,' Polly said gently and her tone was such a contrast to the rush of emotions which had hit him that Elliot couldn't help reacting.

'It showed up on one of the scans.' Elliot tried his best, he really did, but it was impossible to keep the anger out of his voice. 'And if Joseph's mother had had her way then he wouldn't be here now.'

'Really!' Polly exclaimed, unable to hide her surprise. 'You mean that she wanted a termination?'

'Yes. Marianna couldn't handle the thought of having a child that wasn't perfect,' he replied harshly. Polly had the impression that he was struggling to regain control, but it was obvious that he was finding it difficult. There was anger in his voice when he continued and her heart ached for him. 'The only thing she wanted was to get rid of the baby as quickly as possible.'

'So how did you manage to persuade her to keep it?' she said gently, wishing there was a way to comfort him. She sighed softly because, even though they had met only that day, she knew that he wouldn't welcome her sympathy.

'By offering her the one thing guaranteed to make her change her mind: money.' He laughed and she flinched when she heard the bitterness in his voice. 'I paid my ex-wife to have Joseph. And I've never regretted it either.'

Polly didn't know what to say. Elliot had *paid* Joseph's mother to go through with the pregnancy? The thought of how traumatic it must have been for him to do that brought tears to her eyes but she blinked them away. It wouldn't help him if she gave in to her emotions.

'It must have been a very difficult time for you,' she said, struggling to strike the right note, not an easy thing to do when she felt so shaken by what he had told her.

He shrugged. 'It's all water under the bridge now.' He opened the door then glanced back, and Polly felt her heart catch when she saw the pain in his eyes. Maybe he claimed that it no longer mattered but she could tell that it did. 'Any problems then phone me.'

'I will,' she promised, although she doubted if he had heard her as he was already walking to his car. She closed the door, knowing it was pointless standing there to wave him off. That was something else he wouldn't appreciate and it hurt to know how determined he was to distance himself from other people. It was an effort to smile when Joseph looked expectantly at her as she went back to the kitchen. Maybe it had nothing to do with her, but she hated to think of Elliot choosing to lead such a lonely existence.

'Right, young man, what do you usually do at this time of the day?' she said, forcing herself to sound upbeat. The last thing she wanted was to upset Joseph. The thought of his mother not wanting him because he wasn't perfect hurt, but she managed to contain her feelings. 'I imagine you're in school normally but, with it being the Easter holidays, we need to find something to occupy you. What's your favourite way to pass the time?'

'Playing on my games console,' Joseph replied promptly. He spun his chair around and made his way to the huge television set mounted on the wall opposite the sofa. Picking up the remote control, he switched it on then turned on the games console as well. 'Do you know how to play?' he asked hopefully.

'Yes, although I'm not very good,' she admitted, feeling pain stab through her as she picked up the spare controller.

After their parents had been killed in a car crash when Polly was twelve, she and her brother had gone to live with Martin's family. Both sets of parents had been close friends and it had seemed the natural thing to do in the absence of any other family to look after them. Peter and Martin were three years older than Polly, but they had included her in all their games. Even though Peter had moved to New York after he had finished university, he and Martin often played online together. Now she sighed as she sat down on the sofa. She couldn't imagine them playing again after what had happened. Cancelling the wedding was going to have repercussions for a lot of people.

She played for a little while then excused

herself to check on Joseph's medication.
Times and dosages were clearly written down
on the sheet of paper she found in Elliot's
desk, along with the medication itself. Joseph
wasn't due to take anything until lunchtime
so she put everything back in the drawer and
turned to leave, pausing when she caught
sight of a photograph on the shelves behind
the desk. It showed a beautiful blond-haired
woman laughing into the camera. Was this
Joseph's mother? she wondered. Elliot had
referred to her as his *ex*-wife but the fact that
they were divorced didn't mean he wouldn't
have a photograph of her. Even if she had behaved deplorably, it didn't rule out the fact
that he might still have feelings for her.

Polly turned away, surprised by how painful she found that idea. What did it matter if
Elliot was still in love with his ex-wife? It had
nothing to do with her.

'I'll be in my office. Tell the parents I'll speak
to them shortly.'

Elliot left Theatre, not bothering to check
if his instructions had been noted. He simply
expected his staff to do what he said and that
was that. Was he being arrogant, perhaps?

he found himself wondering as he headed to the changing rooms. Polly Davies would have said that he was and the fact that her opinion counted for anything was a source of irritation to him. He had met her only that day so why should he care what she thought?

He showered and dressed then made his way to his office. The previous incumbent had decorated it according to his taste and Elliot was keen to stamp his own mark on it as soon as he could. He cast a disparaging glance at the wall behind the desk, which was filled with photographs of the babies his predecessor had treated. He didn't need pictures to prove he was good at his job and had no intention of carrying on the tradition, although, if he was honest, wouldn't *he* have been glad to see some kind of visible proof that Joseph would survive in the days following his birth?

Elliot's brow furrowed as he sat down. It wasn't like him to start having second thoughts and the fact that he was debating the merits of some old photographs surprised him. Quite frankly, he had been behaving completely out of character ever since that morning and although he wished he could blame it on the accident, he had a feeling that it had more to do with one irritating young woman. Polly Davies had got under his skin and the sooner he got her out again and returned to normal the happier he would be!

Alfie's parents arrived a few minutes later so Elliot pushed all other thoughts out of his head while he dealt with them. He ran through what he had done, outlining the procedure to replace the faulty valve in their baby's heart. The parents had had no warning that anything was wrong so it had been a huge shock for them when Alfie was born and rushed to Theatre. Elliot found that he could relate to how they felt and was less brusque than he might have been normally as he explained that although Alfie was still very poorly, he was hopeful as to the outcome. Sister Thomas smiled approvingly as she ushered the young couple out of the room.

'Thank you, sir. I'm sure Hannah and Ben are very grateful for all you've done.'

Elliot nodded, clamping down on the feeling of warmth that filled him. It was years since he had felt such a connection to a patient and their family and it threw him completely off balance. Was it a good thing? That morning he had decided that he needed to open up a bit but now he wasn't so sure. After all, if he was personally involved in a case then he couldn't remain detached and that was what he had sworn he would do after he and Marianna had divorced. Never again would he allow his emotions to be trampled on. Never again would he fall in love and run the risk of being let down. Oh, he would love Joseph and love him enough to make up for the fact that the boy didn't have a mother, but he wouldn't give his heart to anyone ever again. Was he really prepared to change all that, to open himself up to more heartache?

Elliot took a deep breath then switched on the computer. He would write up his case notes and then he would go home. Home to his son, the only person he needed, the only person he would ever love.

# CHAPTER FOUR

POLLY WAS JUST heating some soup for Joseph's lunch when she heard a car drawing up outside. The morning had flown past as she and Joseph had found various things to do. It turned out that he was an accomplished artist and he had spent some time in the garden drawing a picture of the surrounding countryside. Polly had helped him manoeuvre his chair outside, no easy task as the ground was rather rough. She intended to mention it to Elliot before she left. Now she glanced around when she heard his footsteps coming along the hall.

'Good timing. I've just heated some soup for lunch. There's enough for two so sit yourself down while I fetch Joseph. He's outside, finishing off his picture.'

'Outside?' Elliot's expression darkened as

he glanced towards the garden. 'It's far too cold for him to be out there.'

'Nonsense,' Polly said firmly. 'It's a beautiful day and the fresh air will do him good. It's far better than spending the day in front of a television screen, if you want my opinion.'

'I don't. I shall decide what's best for Joseph, and sitting outside in the cold is the last thing he should be doing.'

He didn't say another word as he strode out of the back door. Polly pulled a face at his retreating back, not caring if it was childish. There was something about Elliot Grey that seemed to bring out the worst in her. She spooned the soup into bowls and set them on the table then took a loaf of bread out of the bread bin. There was butter in the fridge and she put that on the table as well. She had just finished when Joseph came whizzing back into the kitchen and came straight over to her to show her the picture he had drawn.

'I've finished it, Polly. What do you think?' he asked eagerly.

'That you are one very talented little boy.' Bending down, she gave him a hug. 'I absolutely love it, Joseph. It's brilliant, isn't it, Elliot?' she added, glancing up in time to see the strangest expression cross Elliot's face. The best way to describe it was a kind of wistful sadness, although it disappeared so fast that she found herself wondering if she had imagined it.

'Yes, it is. Although, as I said before, Joseph should never have been allowed to sit outside in the first place.'

Joseph's face fell. He didn't say anything else as he manoeuvred his chair next to the table, but Polly could tell how disappointed he was by his father's reaction. Had Elliot really needed to spoil the moment for him by saying that? she thought angrily. It was on the tip of her tongue to remonstrate with him but she knew it would be wrong to say anything in front of Joseph and risk upsetting him even more. She settled instead for pouring Joseph a drink of juice and switching on the kettle, although Elliot could make his own coffee. She certainly didn't intend to stick around and pander to him!

'Right, I'll leave you to it then.' Polly picked up her coat, feeling her heart suddenly sink. Looking after Joseph had proved the perfect distraction but now she needed to think about what she was going to do. It was

only midday and there was still time to catch
the train to London; however, the thought of
spending the coming week wandering around
on her own wasn't appealing, but what choice
did she have? She couldn't face going back
to Martin's parents' house—it would be too
awkward for all of them. There was always
the cottage, of course, but she had no idea if
Martin was planning to stay there once he
came back home. Panic gripped her as the
true precariousness of her situation hit her.
She simply didn't have anywhere to go!

Elliot wasn't sure what was going on but there
was definitely something wrong if the expression on Polly's face was anything to go by.
Even though he knew that he shouldn't get
involved, he couldn't help himself. Walking
around the table, he slid his hand under her
elbow and steered her to a chair. 'Sit down
before you fall down,' he said gruffly because
acting the part of the Good Samaritan didn't
come easily to him. The kettle clicked itself
off so he went to the counter and spooned
instant coffee into a mug. 'Sugar?' he asked,
his heart lurching when Polly stared blankly
back at him.

'Polly doesn't take sugar,' Joseph told him helpfully. 'She just has milk in her coffee.'

'Right. Thank you.' Elliot smiled at his son and Joseph smiled back, making it clear that he had forgiven him for his over-the-top response before. It had been OTT too, Elliot admitted as he went to get the milk from the fridge. Although it was a bit chilly outside, Polly had been right to say that Joseph would gain more from being in the fresh air than being stuck in front of a television screen.

Elliot felt his hand start to shake as he added milk to the mug. It was the first time he had ever conceded that anyone else might be right when it came to what was best for Joseph and it unnerved him. Up till now he had been the one to make all the decisions concerning his son; he had been the one to make all the rules too. And yet here he was, admitting that this woman who he had met only that morning knew more than he did about what was good for Joseph.

The thought disturbed him so much that it was a miracle he didn't spill the coffee as he took it over to the table. He had sworn that he would do his best for Joseph after he was born and that every decision he made would be in his son's best interests too, but what if he had been fooling himself? What if the decisions he had made weren't the best he could have taken? There was only him to make any decisions, after all. Marianna had made it clear from the outset that she'd wanted nothing to do with their child, not when, as she had put it, he was so hideously damaged. Elliot hadn't realised before how much he would have liked to discuss the choices he'd had to make. He had simply done what he had thought was right, but what if he could have consulted someone else, someone like Polly, who saw the situation through fresh eyes?

Elliot took a deep breath, tamping down the panic that threatened to overwhelm him. He mustn't go down that route, no matter how tempting it was. As he knew to his cost, allowing people into his life was a recipe for disaster.

Polly felt her stomach churn as the smell of the coffee hit her. She swallowed hard, afraid that she would embarrass herself even more by throwing up. That Elliot had realised something was wrong was obvious and she hated to think that she was making a fool of herself, only she couldn't help it.

Where *was* she going to live, not just now but in the future? Could she even remain in Beesdale or would she have to move somewhere else? Martin's family were well-known in the town. Martin's father had founded the local solicitor's office, and Martin had gone to work there with him after he had finished university. The firm handled all the legal work in the area and both Martin and his father had a reputation for being completely honest and trustworthy. Although her brother, Peter, had decided that it would be better to tell everyone it had been a mutual decision to cancel the wedding, as Martin had suggested in his letter, would they believe that? After all, she and Martin had known each other for years and there was bound to be a lot of speculation as to why they had decided to call off the wedding at the very last moment. The thought of everyone finding out that Martin had left her for another woman was more than Polly could bear. The last thing she wanted was to be seen as an object of pity!

'Here. Drink this.'

A large hand pushed the mug towards her

and Polly jumped. She had been so lost in her thoughts that she had forgotten where she was for a moment. Picking up the mug, she took a gulp of the coffee then gasped when it scalded her throat.

'Careful!'

The same hand moved the mug out of her reach and she frowned. First he wanted her to drink it and now he didn't—couldn't he make up his mind? Opening her mouth, she went to tell him what he could do with his wretched coffee then suddenly thought better of it. She certainly didn't want to create a scene in front of Joseph.

'If you've finished your lunch then would you mind giving me and Polly a few minutes on our own, Joseph? We need to have a chat and you'll only get bored.'

Polly frowned as she processed what Elliot had said. What did they need to talk about? Surely he wasn't still harping on about her allowing Joseph to go outside, was he? The thought was like the proverbial red rag. Maybe she wouldn't have reacted quite so strongly if she hadn't been feeling so keyed up but, the minute Joseph left the room, she rounded on him. 'If you're still banging on about Joseph going outside—'

'I'm not. You were right. The fresh air probably did him more good than sitting in front of a screen,' Elliot said flatly, stopping her in her tracks.

'Oh. Well, I'm glad you agree,' Polly muttered, not sure what to make of his reply. It seemed so completely out of character for him to admit that she'd been right and he had been wrong that it threw her.

It was left to Elliot to continue, which he did with his customary bluntness. 'It appears that something has upset you. If it was what I said before then I apologise.'

It was another concession she had never expected him to make. Polly stared at him in surprise. 'You're apologising? To *me*?'

'If I'm at fault, then yes.'

'I…ahem…thank you, but it has nothing to do with you.'

Polly stared at her hands as a fresh wave of panic hit her. Even if she did decide to move away, it would take some time to make the necessary arrangements. First of all, she would have to find herself another job so that meant she would have to stay in Beesdale for now. Where was she going to live in the meantime? Perhaps she could go and stay with one of her friends from the surgery, but who exactly? Beth's cottage was tiny and she simply didn't have the room now that she had baby Beatrix to look after. And Ellie and Daniel were busy preparing for the birth of their first child in a couple of months' time. Although Polly knew they would find room for her if she asked them, it didn't seem fair to land herself on them…

'Look, if there's anything I can do to help,' Elliot began then tailed off as though he was already regretting the offer.

'*You?*' Polly didn't mean to sound quite so incredulous but the idea that he would want to help her was laughable.

'Yes, me,' he replied a shade grimly. 'It's obvious that something's upset you so why not tell me what it is? Then we can see if we can put it right.'

'Why?' She stared at him. 'I don't mean to be rude but you don't strike me as the sort of person who's overflowing with the milk of human kindness, so why do you want to help me?'

'Because you helped me this morning by

looking after Joseph.' He shrugged. 'I prefer to pay my debts, so if there's anything I can do then tell me.'

'You don't need to worry,' Polly said flatly, dismissing any ideas she might have been harbouring that he might actually be worried about her. On the contrary, Elliot was simply making sure that she didn't have an excuse to ask him for help in the future. 'As far as I'm concerned there's no debt to repay.'

She stood up abruptly because she wasn't achieving anything by sitting there. She would have to catch the train to London—there was nothing else she could do. The hotel was paid for so at least she had somewhere to stay for the next week. Once she came back, however, it would be a different story. She would have to find somewhere to live, if only for the time it would take to find another job. A sob caught in her throat at the thought of moving away from the town she loved, but she knew it would be the best decision in the long run. Running into Martin all the time, as was bound to happen, would be too difficult, especially if everyone found out that he had ditched her. Folk would wonder why she hadn't realised what had been going on and she couldn't bear to think that she would become the subject of gossip. No, it would be better if she left—better for her, better for everyone.

Polly's heart was heavy as she made her way along the hall. It had been a day for shocks and changes and it was hard to imagine that life would get better. Joseph was in the sitting room and he came rushing out in his wheelchair when he heard her.

'You aren't leaving, are you, Polly? I thought we could play another game this afternoon,' he said when she paused.

'I wish I could, sweetheart, but I have to catch the train.' Bending, she kissed him on the cheek, feeling her emotions bubbling up to the surface. Even though she had met him only that day, she had already grown fond of him. He was such a plucky little boy, making light of his disability in a way that she found both touching and humbling. She tousled his hair, forcing back the ready tears. 'Maybe your dad will play with you.'

'Maybe,' Joseph muttered, making it clear that he didn't hold out any hopes that he would.

Polly glanced at Elliot and raised her brows. 'I'm sure you can fit in a game, can't you?'

'We'll see.' Reaching past her, he opened the door, making it clear that he was keen for her to leave. 'Thank you for minding Joseph. I appreciate it.'

'It wasn't a problem,' Polly replied politely. She walked down the path and got into her car, not looking back before she drove away. She couldn't imagine that Elliot was waiting to wave her off. Now that she had served her purpose, he must be glad to see the back of her. Just for a moment her heart ached at the thought of the lonely life he was creating for himself before common sense reasserted itself. It was his choice and he had to live with it, the same as she had to live with any decisions she made about her future.

'It was Maureen in the store who saw them. Holding hands, they were, in the middle of the street and her due to get married that very day. If you ask me, there's more to them calling off the wedding than they're letting on!'

Polly paused in the doorway to The Larches surgery. It was two weeks since the wedding had been cancelled and she had hoped that people would have found something else to talk about by now, but apparently not. Mrs Barnsthwaite was in full flow, regaling Marie, the receptionist, with what her friend supposedly had seen. Polly had no idea where the story had sprung from; it was just one of many that she'd heard since she had got back from London. It made her see that she was right to start looking for another job. It would be impossible to continue living here when everyone was gossiping about her.

Taking a deep breath, Polly walked over to the reception desk, seeing the embarrassment on Marie's face when she spotted her. Mrs Barnsthwaite took one look at her and hurried away, probably eager to regale someone else with the latest version of the tale. Polly dredged up a smile, deciding it was better to say something rather than pretend she hadn't heard. As her brother, Peter, had insisted on telling her before he had flown back to New York, she had nothing to feel guilty about.

'Another theory as to why we called off the wedding, I take it? That must be the third or fourth version I've heard since I got home. At least it's given everyone something to talk about.'

'I'm so sorry, Polly. I did try to stop her but you know what she's like once she gets going.' Marie sighed. 'I just wish folk would let it drop. OK, so it was a shock, but you and Martin wouldn't have changed your minds if you hadn't had a really good reason.'

'Thanks, Marie.' Polly smiled at the other woman. 'It's nice to know someone's on my side. I feel as though I should be walking about with a bell hanging around my neck, shouting "unclean!"'

'Well, you shouldn't is all I can say.' Marie came around the desk and gave her a hug. 'If there's anything I can do to help, love, then just tell me. OK?'

'I will.' Polly felt her eyes well with tears and turned away before she ended up making a show of herself. However, it was good to know that the people she worked with were on her side.

Daniel was just coming out of his room and he stopped when he saw her coming along the corridor. 'How are you, Polly? Marie said you'd be in this morning to take the antenatal clinic.'

'I'm OK. I'm just going to concentrate on

work and hope that everyone finds something else to talk about soon,' she explained wryly.

'You mustn't let it get to you,' Daniel said gently. 'Oh, I know it was a shock for a lot of folk but it was your and Martin's decision and no one else's. If you thought it was the right thing to do then Eleanor and I are behind you all the way.'

'Thank you. That means a lot, believe me,' Polly murmured as Daniel sketched her a wave and carried on.

She made her way to the room where the clinics were held and started to get set up. Although she visited a lot of her mums at home, those who lived near the town preferred to come to the clinic. They could be checked and weighed then have a chat with the other mums. Polly also held classes to help prepare them for the birth and they were extremely popular and always fully subscribed. She was holding one that morning so, once she had checked the scales, she laid out the mats they would use to relax on. She had just finished when Leah Culthorpe, the new practice nurse, popped her head round the door.

'Oh, so you are here. I thought I'd better

check that the clinic was going ahead,' Leah declared.

'Of course it is. How many have arrived so far?'

'About a dozen.' Leah shrugged. 'More than usual, but I suppose that's to be expected in the circumstances.'

Polly sighed under her breath. They both knew that people would be eager to see her in the hope that they could get an inside track on the gossip, although it would have been more tactful if Leah hadn't made that comment. 'Everything's ready so you may as well show the first one in,' Polly said evenly, letting it pass.

Leah disappeared and a few seconds later the first mum arrived. Polly said hello and got straight down to work, making it clear that the only subject under discussion was the patient's health and that of her unborn child. She wasn't going to say anything about all those silly rumours, like the one she'd heard that morning about her holding hands with some man

Polly gasped as it hit her that there was some truth in it. She'd held Elliot Grey's hand—well, held his wrist, actually. Obviously, Maureen, who worked in the store, had seen them and had got the completely wrong idea. Polly swallowed her groan. All she could do was hope that Elliot wouldn't get wind of it. She couldn't imagine that he would be pleased to be cast in the role of the other man!

# CHAPTER FIVE

'I SEE POLLY'S BACK.'

'Really! Have you seen her?'

'Yes, she's in reception. I must say I was surprised to see her. I don't think I'd be keen to show my face if I'd done what everyone's saying she did…'

The rest of the conversation was swallowed up as the two nurses stepped into the lift Elliot had just vacated. He frowned as he made his way along the corridor. It was two weeks since Polly had looked after Joseph that day and he'd not had sight nor sound of her since. He had assumed that there'd been no reason for her to visit the hospital but it seemed he might have been mistaken. What on earth had she done to deserve a comment like that? he wondered as he pushed open the door to Outpatients. From what he knew of her, Polly wasn't the kind of person to make enemies.

On the contrary, she drew people to her—as he knew from experience.

The thought sent a frisson scudding through him and he sighed as he went into the examination room set aside for his use. Far too often, he had found himself thinking about Polly lately. There was something about her that had stirred his emotions in a way that hadn't happened for a very long time. More than once when he had been speaking to the parents of one of his young patients, he had found himself wondering if she would have approved, and it was galling to say the least. He didn't need anyone's blessing about the way he behaved!

A knock on the door roused him from such unsettling thoughts. He looked up as Donna Roberts came into the room.

'Morning,' the staff nurse said cheerfully, placing a pile of folders on the desk in front of him. 'We've a really long list this morning, starting with little Alfie Nolan's parents. I believe you asked to speak to them before they take Alfie home.'

'That's right.' Elliot reached for the top folder, although he could remember every detail of the case. For some reason it had lodged in his brain, which didn't always happen. Was it the fact that he had met Polly that day that had made it so memorable? he wondered, then immediately dismissed the thought. Not everything that happened could be classified as BP or AP—*before* or *after* Polly!

'Show them in. The sooner we get started, the sooner we'll be finished.' Elliot set the notes aside, determined to put all thoughts of Polly out of his head. She had helped him out of a difficult situation and that was it. Their relationship—such as it was—had started and ended that same day. She wasn't a factor in his life, nor did he intend her to become one. He had Joseph and his work: he had everything he needed...

*Didn't he?*

'Just try to stay calm, Amy. You won't do yourself or your baby any good by getting so worked up.'

Polly patted Amy Carmichael's hand but she could tell that her words were having little effect. Amy had been inconsolable ever since she had received a letter asking her to attend the Outpatients' department. She had been in tears when she had come into the antenatal clinic, which was why Polly had offered to go with her. Amy's husband was in the Army and he was away on tour at the moment. With no other family members living nearby, she was very much on her own. Although it should have been her day off that day, Polly found it easier if she kept busy.

Now that Peter had gone home she felt very much on her own, especially as she was living so far out of town. Peter had managed to find her a cottage as a temporary stopgap and she was grateful to have somewhere to live, even if it was off the beaten track. It was Peter who had fetched her belongings from Martin's parents' house too. They had taken it all very badly and Polly still hadn't spoken to them, although she knew that she would have to do so at some point. She hadn't spoken to Martin either, although she had heard that he was back in Beesdale. She had decided that she would leave it to him to get in touch if he wanted to, although there was very little to say in the circumstances. Cancelling the wedding had caused a great deal of upset and, even though it hadn't been her doing, she couldn't help feeling slightly guilty. It didn't help that the rumours about her and

Elliot were still circulating. Even though she knew there wasn't a scrap of truth in them, it was very hard to swallow. She sighed softly. She just had to hold onto the thought that it wouldn't be long before she moved away and put it all behind her.

'How about a cup of tea?' she suggested now, trying not to think about the forthcoming move. It was what she needed to do to get her life back on track and there was no point getting upset about it.

'I don't think I could drink it.' Amy bit her lip. 'There's something wrong with the baby, isn't there? I thought there was when I had that scan. It was the way that radiographer looked at me.'

She started to sob and Polly put her arm around her and hugged her. 'Let's wait until you've seen the doctor,' she began then stopped when one of the nurses appeared and called Amy's name. 'Do you want me to come in with you, love, or would you prefer to see the consultant on your own?'

'Will you come with me? I don't want to be on my own if it's bad news,' Amy said, wiping her eyes.

'Of course.' Polly slipped her hand under

Amy's elbow and helped her to her feet. They followed the nurse along the corridor to one of the examination rooms. Tapping on the door, the nurse ushered them inside.

'Amy Carmichael, sir.'

'Thank you.'

Polly bit back a gasp when the man swung his chair around and she realised it was Elliot Grey. It had never crossed her mind that he would see patients in clinic. His predecessor hadn't done so, leaving it to his registrar, so it was a shock to see Elliot sitting there. In a fast sweep, her eyes ran over him, her heart sinking as she took stock once more of that air of aloofness he projected. He hadn't changed, although she had no idea why she had imagined that he would have done. After all, what reason was there to think that meeting her might have made a difference to him? The truth was that she had made no impact whatsoever on him and it hurt to realise it, hurt in a way she couldn't understand either. After what had happened, it would be a long time before she was ready for another relationship.

'Please sit down.'

Elliot cleared his throat and Polly had

the distinct impression that he was as disconcerted to see her as she was to see him. Heat flashed along her veins as she drew up a chair, wondering why it made her feel so on edge to know that he wasn't indifferent to her after all. She had to force herself to concentrate when he continued.

'I asked to see you today, Mrs Carmichael, because your ultrasound scan has shown that your baby has a diaphragmatic hernia,' he said without any preamble.

'A hernia,' Amy repeated, barely able to get the words out. Polly set aside her own feelings, knowing what a shock this must be for her, even though Amy had feared the worst.

'That is correct. Basically, what it means is that some of the baby's abdominal contents are in the place where his lungs should be and this is affecting how his lungs develop,' Elliot continued.

'Does it mean that he can't breathe properly?' Amy asked, tears starting to trickle down her face again.

'At the moment your baby doesn't use his lungs because he's receiving oxygenated blood from the placenta via his umbilical cord,' Elliot explained. 'However, once he's born and needs to start breathing properly, it could become a problem. It depends how much of his lungs have been damaged.'

'Are you saying that he could die?' Amy exclaimed. She turned to Polly, her face mirroring her horror. 'Is that what's going to happen—my baby's going to die because he can't breathe?'

'No, Amy, he isn't,' Polly said quickly. 'There will be a team of doctors and nurses there when he's born and they will help him to breathe. Isn't that right, Dr Grey?'

'Yes. I, along with my colleagues, will be present at the birth and we shall intubate and ventilate your baby.'

'Basically, what that means is that a tube will be inserted into your baby's windpipe so that he can be given oxygen,' Polly explained gently because she could tell that Amy had no idea what Elliot meant.

'And you can do that at my house?' Amy asked uncertainly.

'No. It will need to be done here in the hospital,' Elliot told her.

'But I want to have my baby at home!' Amy wailed, getting even more upset at the thought of being admitted to the hospital. She turned beseechingly to Polly. 'Surely you can sort it out, Polly. You can help my baby breathe, can't you?'

'I'm afraid I can't, Amy. I simply don't have the necessary expertise.' Polly patted the young mum's hand. 'I know how disappointed you must be when you were planning to have a home birth, but the baby's safety comes first. He's going to need a lot of care after he's born and he can only receive that here in the hospital.'

She glanced at Elliot when a distraught Amy started to sob in earnest and was surprised to see what looked like sympathy in his eyes. Maybe he wasn't as unfeeling as he appeared, she thought, and felt a rush of pleasure at the idea. It was a moment before she realised that he was speaking.

'I understand that this must be a shock for you, Mrs Carmichael, but we have to put your baby's welfare first. Once he's been ventilated he will be moved to the neonatal unit, where he will continue to receive support with his breathing.'

Elliot's tone was calm to the point of being emotionless as he explained that the hole in the baby's diaphragm would be surgically repaired, although it wasn't possible to predict the outcome at this stage as it depended on the amount of healthy lung tissue that remained. Polly felt her momentary rush of euphoria fade. Far from being filled with compassion for poor Amy, Elliot obviously viewed this as just another case. He didn't really care about the people involved or the effect it would have on them.

It was a dispiriting thought and it was a relief when he brought the interview to a conclusion. Polly helped Amy to her feet, trying not to let her disappointment show as she bade Elliot goodbye. How could he be so unfeeling? she wondered as she and Amy made their way along the corridor. Surely he, more than anyone, understood how devastating it was to find out that your baby wasn't perfect? She had seen the expression on his face when he had told her about Joseph and knew that he had been as upset as any parent would have been in such circumstances, yet he seemed unable to take those feelings and translate them into compassion for anyone else…unable or *unwilling*?

Polly frowned as she glanced back along the corridor. Was that the real explanation?

It wasn't that Elliot didn't feel anything but that he didn't *allow* himself to feel it? He had locked away his emotions and refused to admit that he possessed any. Polly knew it was true and her heart ached even more because he wasn't only cutting himself off from other people: he was cutting himself off from his real self.

Elliot felt on edge for the rest of the day. He was in Theatre that afternoon and far too often he found himself thinking about what had happened that morning when he had seen Polly. He was very aware that he had fallen far short of her expectations when he had broken the news to Amy Carmichael, but what else could he have done? Amy needed to understand the facts of the situation and he would have been doing her a huge disservice if he had tried to pretend that everything would be fine, although maybe he could have been a bit more positive about the eventual outcome.

He sighed as he thanked his team and left Theatre. It wasn't like him to wonder if he had done the right thing but for some reason Polly seemed to have this effect on him. He had always believed that it was better not to let emotions get in the way but she obviously didn't share that view. She had done everything she could to make it easier for Amy but, as he knew from experience, nobody could take away the pain of learning that your child wasn't perfect. It was something you had to come to terms with, as he'd had to come to terms with his own pain over Joseph.

Marianna hadn't stayed around after Joseph was born. Although Elliot had hoped that she might change her mind once she saw him, she had refused to have anything to do with him, so there had been nobody to share the heartache with. Every parent expected to have a perfect child and it was hard to accept that your child was never going to be that. Would it have helped if he'd been able to talk through his feelings? he mused then immediately dismissed the idea. As he knew to his cost, there was no point relying on other people: they only let you down.

It was a sobering thought but it helped to put things into perspective. Elliot drove home, feeling his spirits lift as he left the city behind. The Yorkshire Dales really was a beautiful part of the world, he thought as

he drove along the winding roads to Beesdale. He reached the outskirts of the town and
paused at the crossroads. He rarely drank alcohol but, after the day he'd had, he could do
with a glass of wine—he would stop off at the
shops and treat himself to a bottle. He turned
left and parked in the High Street. There was
a very good general store there that sold wine,
along with everything else.

The old-fashioned brass bell jingled mer-
rily as he opened the door and made his way
to the small but well-stocked off-licence section. There were a couple of women standing at the till, chatting, but it wasn't until he
heard Polly's name mentioned that he paid
any attention.

'I still can't believe it. I mean, I really like
Polly—she delivered my youngest grand-
son and my daughter can't speak too highly
of her. But to be carrying on with another
man— Well!'

'I know. It was a dreadful thing to do—'

The bell jangled as someone else came into
the store and the conversation stopped dead.
Elliot frowned as he took a bottle of wine
off the shelf. It was the second time that day
he'd heard someone talking about Polly in

less than complimentary terms. What had they meant about her carrying on with another man? He wouldn't have put her down as the unfaithful type but, there again, what exactly did he know about her? A feeling of intense disappointment swept over him. For all he knew, Polly could have a string of lovers on the go!

Elliot turned to make his way to the till, stopping abruptly when Polly herself suddenly appeared at the end of the aisle. She stopped when she saw him and he had the distinct impression that she was about to turn tail and run. Maybe it was curiosity that got the better of him, but he realised that he couldn't let her leave without finding out what was going on. Foolish or not, but it seemed important to find out if Polly really was the person he had thought her to be.

'Are you after a bottle of wine as well to round off a busy day?' he asked lightly, stunned by the fact that it should matter so much.

'Erm…yes.' Reaching out, she grabbed the first bottle she came to, and Elliot's brows rose.

'Champagne? Are you celebrating?'

'No, of course not.' Colour flooded her face as she put the bottle back on the shelf and reached for another one. 'This will do,' she said, picking up a bottle of Pinot Grigio.

'Snap.' Elliot held up the bottle he'd chosen so she could see the label. 'Obviously, we have the same taste in wine.'

'So it seems.'

She gave him a thin smile as she edged past him but Elliot was unwilling to let her escape so easily. Maybe it was the fact that he'd had such a miserable afternoon thanks to her, combined with all those snippets of conversation he'd overheard, but he found himself hurrying after her. The two women were still standing by the till and he saw them look at one another when he appeared. He had a feeling that he was missing something, although he had no idea what it could be.

He waited while Polly paid for her wine then handed over a ten pound note and paid for his, conscious of the silence that had fallen. The shop bell rang and he snatched up the bottle, determined to get to the bottom of the mystery. Polly was already unlocking her car when he got outside and he hurried over to where she had parked. Maybe it had nothing to do with him what she had done, but it made no difference. He wanted to know what she was guilty of. Needed to know for some reason he couldn't explain. Up until today, he had thought she was perfect— kind, caring, considerate, *faithful*. However, it appeared the picture he had built of her wasn't true. If the gossip was to be believed, Polly wasn't perfect after all. She had flaws, just like every other woman he had known, and he needed to get that clear in his head. Maybe then he could stop entertaining all these crazy thoughts and get back to normal. Once he knew her for who she really was, she would lose her appeal. And that was what he wanted more than anything.

Polly could feel her hands shaking as she opened the car door. There was no doubt in her mind that she had been the topic of conversation in the store tonight. That would have been bad enough, but she had seen the way Maureen had looked at Elliot and knew that she had recognised him as the man in the car—the man she supposedly had jilted Martin for.

How long would it be before Elliot heard

the story? she wondered sickly. Gossip spread like wildfire in a small town like Beesdale and it wouldn't be long before he found himself the topic of conversation. The thought of him being drawn into this mess made her grow hot with embarrassment. She could just imagine his reaction!

'You're in a hurry. Going somewhere special tonight?'

The sound of his deep voice behind her made her jump and the bottle of wine slipped through her fingers and smashed on the ground. Wine spattered her feet and she let out a little cry of surprise. 'Oh!'

'Hell!' All of a sudden Elliot was beside her, moving her out of the way as he bent down and picked up the pieces of broken glass. 'I am so sorry,' he said, dumping the glass into a nearby litter bin. 'That was my fault for startling you. If you give me a second, I'll go and buy you another bottle.'

'No!' Polly took a quick breath when she heard the panic in her voice but she had to stop him from going back into the store. What if Maureen said something to him? she thought sickly. What if she asked him about the rumours that were circulating? It was the last thing a man in Elliot's position would want. Not only did he have his reputation as a surgeon to consider but there was Joseph and how it could impact on him if he heard what was being said. Even though she hated the idea, Polly knew that she had to warn him what was going on.

'It doesn't matter,' she said huskily, trying to decide how to begin. Would it be better to lead up to it gently, make a joke out of all those rumours? she wondered then immediately dismissed the idea. From what she knew of Elliot, he wouldn't find anything the least bit amusing about this situation.

'Look, I don't know if you noticed a certain…well, atmosphere in the store tonight,' she began, feeling her way.

'You mean when we got to the till?' he said bluntly and her heart sank. Obviously, he had noticed something strange so she couldn't ignore it: she would have to explain.

'Erm…yes. I know you're going to find this completely ridiculous but there are certain rumours going around.'

'What sort of rumours?'

'About me,' she muttered, her tongue

tripping over her teeth in embarrassment. 'And you.'

'Really? I can't imagine what kind of rumours you mean.' One dark brow arched questioningly although his expression gave away very little about his feelings.

Polly took a deep breath, knowing that she had to go on even though it was the last thing she felt like doing. 'It appears that people have got it into their heads that we—you and me, I mean—are an item.'

'And why would they think that?'

'Because of what happened the day we met.' Polly could feel her heart thumping, *bang, bang, bang* like a big bass drum. She didn't want to tell him about Martin and her cancelled wedding. Elliot didn't have a very high opinion of her already because of her job and if she told him about Martin dumping her then he would start to wonder what was wrong with her...

'And what did happen, apart from you looking after Joseph?' he prompted in a voice that told her there was no way he would let her stop now. He intended to hear the whole story, every little detail, and her heart sank because she knew the damage it would cause.

'That day…the day of the accident…I was supposed to be getting married.' Polly could hear the words but they didn't seem to be coming from her lips. It was as though she was listening to someone else saying them because they didn't have any impact. It wasn't what she was saying that mattered, she realised, but how Elliot was going to react to it.

'*Supposed* to be getting married,' he repeated, staring at her.

'Yes. But he…I mean we…called it off,' she said hurriedly, wondering if it would have been better to tell him the truth, that Martin had dumped her for another woman. However, it was done now and she had no choice but to carry on. 'I don't want to go into the whys and wherefores. I'm sure you aren't interested in all that, but somehow people have got it into their heads that we cancelled the wedding because I'd met someone else…' She tailed off, unable to tell him the final bit, the bit she knew he was going to hate.

'Who?'

Polly blanched when he shot the question at her. She knew there was no way that she could avoid answering it, no way that he would let her. Taking a deep breath, she lifted her head, seeing the dawning anger in his eyes.

'You.'

# CHAPTER SIX

'WAIT IN HERE. I need to check on Joseph first.'

Elliot opened the sitting room door then stepped aside while Polly made her way into the room. He couldn't remember the last time he had felt this angry. People were gossiping about him and Polly? Blaming *him* for her dumping her fiancé? Quite frankly, he was entitled to feel angry and a whole lot more!

He made his way up the stairs, pausing at the top while he took a deep breath. He didn't want Joseph to think there was anything wrong, didn't want his son becoming involved in this fiasco in any way at all. It could start him wondering if there was any truth in those rumours and that was the last thing Elliot wanted. Joseph had made it clear that he liked Polly but he had no idea what she was really like—that she was exactly the same as his mother. Marianna had had affairs too, several of them during the time they had been married. She had been incapable of being faithful and not just to him either but to her own child. He wasn't about to allow another woman like that into Joseph's life!

'Hi.' He opened the bedroom door, feeling his insides churning with all the emotions that had gripped him since Polly had told him what was going on. For the past eight years he had refused to allow himself to feel very much but he couldn't seem to control his feelings now. Of course he was angry. And upset. And worried to death about the effect it could have on Joseph if he heard the rumours. However, worse than all of that, he felt bitterly disappointed. Somewhere along the line, he had placed Polly on a pedestal and what a mistake that had been. Polly was no better than all the other women he had known. No better than his mother, who had ruined his father's life by sleeping with his business partner, no better than Marianna, who had slept with whoever she had wanted. Polly was the same as them. No kinder. No more caring. Definitely not more faithful! It hurt to face the truth when it was so bitterly unpalatable.

'Hi, Dad. You're late. Did something happen so you had to stay at the hospital?'

Joseph smiled up at him and Elliot's heart ached all the more. He knew that Joseph was waiting to hear all about what had delayed him but this was one subject he had no intention of discussing with him.

'I was in Theatre,' he explained, fudging the truth. If he told Joseph that he had run into Polly it would only arouse his interest. Joseph kept asking when he could see her again but, after tonight's revelations, Elliot was determined that it was never going to happen. 'It just took longer than I thought to get through the list.'

'Oh, I see.' Joseph gave a little shrug as he turned his attention back to the book he was reading and Elliot breathed a sigh of relief that he had got away with it. Bending, he kissed Joseph on the forehead then smiled at him.

'You can read for another ten minutes and then you must put the light out—OK?'

'OK,' Joseph muttered, already engrossed in the story.

Elliot made his way downstairs and headed straight to the kitchen, where Mrs Danton was watching a soap opera on the television. He had failed to find anyone to look after Joseph when he came home from school so Elliot had come to an agreement with his housekeeper. During term time, she would stay with Joseph until Elliot got back from work, although he would have to find someone else to cover during the school holidays as Mrs Danton needed to look after her grandchildren then. He sighed as he saw her out. It was another problem he needed to solve, something more to worry about on top of everything else...

*What on earth was he going to do if Joseph heard those rumours about him and Polly?*

Elliot could feel his temper rising once more as he made his way to the sitting room. Polly was standing by the fireplace and she looked round when he opened the door. Elliot felt a rush of sympathy hit him when he saw how upset she looked but quashed it. She had brought this on herself so why should he waste his sympathy on her? Maybe he wasn't the other party involved but there was no smoke without fire. She deserved everything she got for cheating on her fiancé!

\* \* \*

Polly wasn't sure if it had been a good idea to come back to Elliot's home. She had hoped that they might be able to straighten things out once she had time to talk to him properly. However, one glance at his face showed her just how difficult that was going to be. Oh, she could understand why he was angry: she felt angry too. But she hadn't started those stupid rumours. She was as much a victim of the gossipmongers as he was, although she doubted if he appreciated that fact. As far as Elliot was concerned she was to blame for everything that had happened.

The sheer injustice of it roused her and she rounded on him. 'Look, I know you're upset but it isn't my fault. I didn't start those rumours.'

'Maybe you didn't, but you're the one who was unfaithful.' He smiled thinly, making no attempt to hide his contempt. 'I realise it must be galling for you to be found out but you should have thought of that before, shouldn't you?'

'Unfaithful?' Polly repeated, unable to believe her ears. 'I wasn't *unfaithful* to Martin!'

'No? Then why did he call off the wedding?' Elliot leant against the mantelpiece and regarded her with undisguised cynicism.

'I…erm…it was a…a mutual decision, as I already explained,' she muttered uncomfortably, even though in a way it was true. If Martin had had the courage to tell her what was going on then *she* would have immediately called off the wedding, wouldn't she? For some reason the thought made her feel a little better.

Elliot must have heard the hesitation in her voice, however, because he laughed. 'Really? I have to say that you don't sound too sure about that. Still, I imagine it's hard to come out and admit that you were cheating on the man you had promised to marry.'

'That's not true! It wasn't me who was cheating—it was Martin!' Polly retorted, stung by the taunting note in his voice. Her heart sank when she suddenly realised what she had said but there was no way that she could take back the words now.

'And you really expect me to believe that?' Elliot said sceptically.

'No. I don't expect you to believe anything I say,' Polly said huskily. Maybe it was foolish to get upset but it hurt to know that he didn't believe her when she was telling him the truth.

'So when did you find out what was going on?' he asked.

Polly shivered when she realised that his tone sounded less confrontational this time. Was it a sign that he was willing to listen to her? Listen and possibly believe? Hope rose inside her, even though she wasn't sure why it mattered so much what he thought. 'The night before the wedding. Martin left me a letter, telling me that he had met someone else and wanted to be with her.'

'He left you a *letter*?' Elliot said incredulously. 'You mean he didn't tell you in person?'

'No. I haven't seen or spoken to him.' She felt the ready tears sting her eyes but, now that she had come this far, she had to tell Elliot the rest. 'When Martin didn't phone me as we'd arranged the night before the wedding, I realised something must be wrong and drove over to the cottage we'd bought. Martin wasn't there but he'd left the letter on the mantelpiece in the sitting room.'

The tears spilled over then, pouring down her face as she recalled the shock she'd had.

Why had she never realised that Martin hadn't really loved her? she thought. Had her desire to get married and have a stable family life affected her judgement to such an extent that she had ignored the warning signs? After all, there'd been many evenings when Martin had claimed he'd had to work late, but had it been true or had he been seeing this other woman? With the benefit of hindsight, Polly knew it was so and it hurt to know how stupid she had been. When Elliot put his hand under her arm and led her to a chair, she didn't protest.

'You're well rid of him, from the sound of it,' he said harshly as he sat her down, but Polly sensed that his anger was no longer directed at her. For some reason, she found the idea comforting.

'That's what my brother said,' she told him, dredging up a watery smile. 'Peter told me that I'd had a lucky escape.'

'He was right too.' Crouching down in front of her, he looked into her eyes. 'Nobody deserves to be treated so callously, Polly. You definitely don't.'

Polly felt her breath catch when she saw the way he was looking at her with such con-

cern. All of a sudden all the hurt and humil-
iation she had felt ever since she had found
that letter started to fade away. Maybe she
should have realised what was going on but
she wasn't to blame; it was Martin who was
at fault for deceiving her.

'You will get over this, Polly. Oh, I know
it probably doesn't feel as though you will
right now, but once you've had time to come
to terms with what's happened then you'll be
able to put it behind you.'

'Do you really think so?' she whispered,
grateful for his reassurance.

'I know so.' He squeezed her fingers. 'I
thought I'd never get over Joseph's mother
abandoning him but I did.'

'It left its mark, though,' she said softly,
and he sighed.

'Every experience—good or bad—affects
us in some way. It's how we deal with what
happens that counts. You'll put all this behind
you in time and get on with your life.'

'As you've got on with your life.'

'Yes. I had to because I had to think about
Joseph and what was best for him. Maybe
there are things I wish I'd done differently,

but I did what I thought was right. For both of us.'

'Is that why you distance yourself from other people?' she asked, holding her breath. She knew she was crossing a lot of boundaries by asking him that. Elliot wasn't a man who discussed his feelings with anyone and it was a lot to expect him to open up to her.

'I find it easier not to get emotionally involved,' he said bluntly. 'It means I can focus on Joseph's needs. Making sure he's safe and happy is my only concern.'

'I can understand that but it must be lonely at times, surely?' she said gently, her heart aching. Elliot had put his own life on hold so that he could concentrate on his son and, whilst it was an admirable thing to do in a way, she wasn't convinced it was the best thing for him or for Joseph.

'I don't have time to be lonely,' he said flatly. 'Between my work and taking care of Joseph, my days are full.'

'But surely you need more than that, something for *you* personally,' she countered.

'If you mean another relationship then, no, I don't. After what happened with Joseph's mother, I'm not interested in having a relationship with anyone else.' His brows rose. 'What about you? Are you keen to try again after what's happened to you?'

She shook her head. 'No. It will take some time before I think about anything like that.'

'Then it appears we're both in the same boat. Both casualties of love, if love is really what it was, which I very much doubt,' he added cynically.

Polly felt a knot of pain twist her heart. It hurt to know that Elliot no longer believed in love, although she had no idea why. It was a relief when he changed the subject back to what they had been discussing earlier.

'So what are you going to do about those rumours that are going around?' he asked, standing up. 'I certainly don't want Joseph to hear them and get the wrong idea.'

'What can I do?' Polly sighed. 'If I kick up a fuss then folk will only think there's some truth to what's being said.'

'So your plan—if one can call it that—is to do nothing?' He shook his head. 'It's not good enough, I'm afraid.'

'So what do you suggest?' she said sharply, standing up. After the way he had treated her with such compassion moments earlier, it was doubly upsetting to have him revert to his old ways. 'Put an advert in the local paper to the effect that you and I are not having an affair and that, contrary to popular belief, I didn't dump Martin for you?'

'Of course not. Don't be ridiculous!'

He swung round, looming over her in a way that made Polly's heart lurch. All of a sudden she was aware of him in a way she hadn't been before, aware of how tall he was, how warm his body felt, how good he smelled, a combination of clean fresh skin and adult male... Her eyes rose and she felt her breath catch when she saw the way he was looking at her so intently. Was Elliot aware of her too? she thought giddily. Aware of the heat of her body, the scent of her skin? Aware that it would take only the tiniest movement to reach out and touch her?

The thought had barely crossed her mind when he did exactly that, reached out and grasped her arm. Polly could feel the heat of his hand seeping through her skin and gasped. How could he make her feel this way—hot and aching—just by a touch? How could he arouse her desire without even trying? She had no idea what the answer was but maybe it was the need to find out that made her lean towards him, even though it wasn't a conscious decision.

Her body came to rest against his and she felt the fire inside her grow even hotter. Could Elliot feel it too? she wondered, staring into his set face. Feel the heat and the desire growing stronger, or was he immune to her nearness? A shudder ran through her when she felt his body suddenly stir to life. When he bent towards her, Polly didn't move. She simply stood there, waiting for the moment when his mouth would claim hers. What would happen after that was unknown, but it didn't matter what happened in the future. It was this kiss that mattered, the first touch of his mouth on hers, the first taste of his lips...

A loud crash from upstairs broke the spell. Elliot didn't utter a word as he pushed her away from him but he didn't need to. Polly could tell from his expression how he felt and her heart ached. It wasn't right that he should feel such remorse because he had wanted to kiss her. For once in his life, he had allowed his emotions to lead the way and she knew that he wouldn't let it happen again, that he would redouble his efforts to remain detached. She bit her lip to hold back the wave of sadness that engulfed her. That kiss which had promised so much had done untold damage.

Joseph was lying on the floor, crying, when Elliot went into his room. He scooped him up and laid him gently back on the bed, feeling his heart racing. Fear that his son had hurt himself had combined with a sense of self-loathing. He had come within a hair's breadth of kissing Polly and he would regret it until his dying day. Polly was the last woman he should get involved with. She had baggage—truckloads of baggage!—and he needed to stay well away from her. He knew all that and yet in another second he would have kissed her and kept on kissing her too. What was wrong with him? Why was he behaving this way? Was he having some sort of crisis because he had given up the life he knew in London and moved here? Or was the explanation even less complicated than that? After all, it had been months since he had slept with a woman, so wasn't it more likely that it had been a natural response to her nearness?

'Is everything all right?'

Elliot spun round, his stomach knotting with tension when he saw Polly standing in the doorway. Try as he might, he couldn't hold onto the idea that it had been the lack of sex that had been the trigger for his actions. It was Polly he had wanted to kiss and no other woman would have done. The minute he'd felt her body against his, his desire had awoken. How or why she had this effect on him, he didn't know, but there was no point trying to deny it. On the contrary, he needed to face up to how he felt and accept how vulnerable he was where she was concerned. Maybe then he wouldn't make the same mistake again.

'Polly! I didn't know you were here.'

The excitement in Joseph's voice brought Elliot back to the present with a rush and his mouth thinned. The last thing he wanted was Joseph reading anything into the fact that Polly was here in their house. Maybe she wasn't responsible for calling off her wedding as those rumours claimed, but she definitely had major issues to deal with at the moment. There was no way that he wanted to risk Joseph growing attached to her so the less contact his son had with her the better...

The less contact *he* had with her too, the better it would be, Elliot amended hurriedly.

'I only popped in for a few minutes,' Polly said quietly as she walked over to the bed. 'So what happened? That was quite a thud, young man.'

'I was trying to reach my tablet and fell out of bed,' Joseph explained, his tears forgotten. 'I didn't hurt myself though 'cos I landed on the rug.'

'Well, that's good to know. You landed with such a thump that I thought the ceiling was going to fall in. It may very well do so the next time so you'd better be careful in future.'

Joseph laughed, forgetting the fright he'd had. Elliot was very aware that he would have handled things differently and that it might not have had the same effect either. Would it have been better to lecture Joseph about the need to take more care or was Polly's way, making a joke of what had happened, best after all? It was hard to decide and his own indecision annoyed him. He didn't enjoy having doubts about his parenting skills!

'So long as you're sure you didn't hurt yourself then it's time you went to sleep.'

He bent down and kissed Joseph, reluctantly moving aside so Polly could kiss him as well.

'Night, night, sleep tight,' she murmured, ruffling Joseph's hair. 'Mind the bed bugs don't bite.'

'That's funny.' Joseph grinned up at her. 'Did you make it up?'

'No. It's something my mummy used to say to me when I was a little girl.'

'I don't have a mummy,' Joseph told her, solemnly. 'She didn't want me 'cos my legs don't work properly.'

Elliot was appalled. Whenever Joseph had asked about his mother, he had told him that she lived in another country and that was why they didn't see her. He'd had no idea that Joseph had worked out the truth for himself and didn't know what to say. He glanced at Polly and could tell how shocked she was too. No wonder, he thought grimly. Very few women would have rejected their own child so callously, the way Marianna had done.

'No more chat,' he said firmly, bending down to kiss Joseph a second time, not that it would make up for his mother abandoning him. His heart was aching as he straightened but he forced himself to smile. 'It's school in the morning, don't forget, and you'll be tired if you don't get to sleep.'

'OK,' Joseph murmured, closing his eyes. He suddenly opened them again and looked at Polly. 'When are you coming to see us again, Polly? Can you come this weekend? Then I can show you the pictures I've drawn. They're really good.'

'I'm not sure, sweetheart.' Polly glanced at him and Elliot found himself holding his breath. He didn't want her making any promises, didn't want her becoming involved in Joseph's life in any way at all. She had suffered a major shock recently and she needed time to get over it. Although spending time with Joseph might fill a gap for her at the moment, she would soon grow tired of being with him. He certainly didn't intend to run the risk of Joseph getting hurt if and when that happened. When Joseph opened his mouth to say something else, Elliot quickly forestalled him.

'That's quite enough for one night, young man. It's time you were asleep so settle down and close your eyes.'

Thankfully, Joseph did as he was told this time, although Elliot guessed it was only a temporary reprieve. Now that Joseph had seen Polly again he would keep asking to see her and it was the last thing Elliot wanted. He followed Polly downstairs, waiting while she fetched her bag from the sitting room. They were both rather subdued as he saw her out but that was to be expected after everything that had happened.

Elliot sighed as he closed the front door and made his way to the kitchen. It had been quite a night, one way and another. Apart from the worry about Joseph growing attached to Polly, there were his own feelings to consider. He had come so close to committing a massive error tonight and there was no way that he wanted to risk it happening again. Oh, maybe he should be able to guarantee it wouldn't now that he understood how vulnerable he was, but it wasn't that simple. There was something about Polly that pressed all his buttons and made him behave completely out of character. Tonight was the perfect example of that. He'd had no intention of kissing her yet the minute he had touched her, it was as though he had turned into someone else, someone who allowed his emotions to dictate his actions, and it scared him. Polly had the ability to disrupt his life as well as

Joseph's and that was why he needed to stay well away from her in the future.

Elliot picked up the bottle of wine he had bought and put it in the fridge because the last thing he needed was alcohol clouding his brain. He had to keep a clear head and recognise the dangers for what they were. The fact was that he couldn't trust himself where Polly was concerned. Maybe Joseph would be disappointed about not seeing her again but he would get over it, as he himself would get over this...this *crush* he seemed to have on her. That was what it was, of course, an infatuation, and nothing more than that. It would soon disappear if he didn't see her.

Elliot switched off the lights and made his way upstairs, deciding he would have an early night. Eight hours' sleep would help to clear his head and set him back on course, he assured himself as he undressed. He slid beneath the duvet and closed his eyes, but sleep proved elusive. When it did finally claim him, his dreams were full of what had happened that night, full of Polly: the scent of her skin; the heat of her body; the sweet promise of her lips...

He came awake with a rush, his heart

pounding, his blood racing through his veins. If this was a crush then it wasn't going to be easy to rid himself of it!

# CHAPTER SEVEN

POLLY FOUND IT impossible to put what had happened out of her mind as she drove home It wasn't only that near-miss kiss that troubled her, although that had been disturbing enough. It was what Joseph had said about his mother. It was hard to believe that the woman didn't want any contact with him because of his disability, yet Polly had seen the anguish on Elliot's face and knew it was true. It made her realise what a difficult time Elliot must have had, caring for Joseph without any support from his mother. It was the ultimate betrayal and she could understand why he was so determined not to let anyone get close to him again. Having been let down so badly, why would he want to risk it happening again?

The thought stayed with her so that she felt tired and drained when she went to work the following morning. Her first appointment was at Applethwaite Farm, where she was going to see Lauren. Lauren and Sam had taken over one of the old farmworkers' cottages and turned it into a comfortable home, independent of Sam's parents, who lived in the main farmhouse. Lauren greeted Polly with a smile when she knocked on the door. She had completely recovered from the operation to remove her appendix and was now fifteen weeks pregnant. She had put on quite a lot of weight and her baby bump was already very noticeable, much to her delight. However, Polly wanted to make sure that Lauren understood it was better not to gain too much weight so soon.

'You've gained another pound since I last weighed you,' she observed, making a note on Lauren's chart. 'Ideally, you should put on between four to six pounds in the first trimester and about a pound per week during the following two trimesters. I want you to be a bit more careful about what you eat, Lauren.'

'I'll try, but my mother-in-law keeps popping over with all sorts of delicious food.' Lauren grimaced. 'It's hard to resist when

it's sitting there in front of you, especially as
Diane is such a wonderful cook.'

'It must be.' Polly laughed ruefully. 'I just
wish someone would pop over with something delicious for me. It's no fun cooking
for one.'

'I'm sure it isn't,' Lauren said sympathetically. 'I was so sorry about you and Martin,
Polly. I always thought you made a lovely
couple but I suppose these things happen.
And if you've met someone else—' Lauren
broke off, looking embarrassed at having said
too much.

Polly sighed. 'So you've heard the rumours
then? All I can say is they're a load of nonsense because there is no one else.'

'But Maureen is going round telling everyone that she saw you with him!' Lauren
exclaimed. 'Has she been making it up? Because if she has then that's an awful thing
to do.'

'I'm sure it wasn't deliberate,' Polly said
hastily, not wanting to cause any trouble. The
last thing she needed was people taking sides.
'Maureen just read more into what she saw
than there actually was. Remember that man

who ran into the back of your van? Well, she saw me with him.'

'He's the one you've been seeing?' Lauren said in surprise.

'Yes. No. What I mean is that he's the one I'm *supposed* to have been seeing,' Polly said, stumbling over her words as she tried to explain.

'But Maureen said you two were holding hands,' Lauren pointed out.

'I was checking his pulse,' Polly corrected her. 'I was worried in case he'd injured himself when he ran into you…' She tailed off, realising how unlikely it sounded even though it was true.

'Oh. Right. Well, I can see how people might have got the wrong idea,' Lauren said gamely, although it was obvious that she was finding it hard to believe the story.

Polly decided to leave it there. She had a nasty feeling that she might end up digging herself an even deeper hole if she said anything else. She finished examining Lauren and left, refusing the cup of coffee she was offered as she didn't want to have to answer any more awkward questions. She did two more home visits and it was clear that the

rumours had reached even the furthest cor-
ners of Beesdale. Polly did her best to pass
them off as nothing more than idle speculation, but she could tell that nobody really believed her. What made it worse was that there
was a mother-and-baby clinic that afternoon
at the surgery which she was taking and she
knew that she would have to run the gauntlet
all over again. Everyone was curious and who
could blame them? Calling off a wedding at
the very last moment wasn't something that
most couples did and folk were bound to want
to know the ins and outs of why she and Martin had taken such a drastic step. She sighed,
knowing there was very little she could do to
stop the gossip. She would just have to put up
with it until she left.

The thought of leaving the place where she
had grown up was a painful one. As she drove
into the surgery car park, Polly realised that
she would miss living here, miss the people
too, even if they did gossip a lot! She turned
off the engine then paused as another thought
struck her: she was going to miss Elliot and
Joseph too. They had become an important
part of her life, even though she wasn't sure
why. It was going to be hard to move away

and not know what happened to them in the future. Although she could probably find out if she kept in touch with her friends at the surgery, what would be the point? Elliot didn't want her in his life and in a way she couldn't blame him. After everything he had been through, it was little wonder that he wasn't interested in having another relationship. He had turned his back on love and she doubted if anyone could change his mind.

It was hard to shake off that thought as she got ready for the afternoon's clinic. Beth Andrews was first through the door. Beth was one of the doctors at The Larches. She was currently on maternity leave and wasn't due to return to work until later in the year. Now she grimaced as she carried baby Beatrix over to the table to be weighed.

'This little madam has been awake since four a.m. I'm shattered even if she's not!'

'The joys of motherhood,' Polly replied, drumming up a laugh. It obviously wasn't convincing because Beth looked at her in concern.

'What's up? It isn't all those stupid rumours, is it? Marie told me about the latest. You wonder how people come up with such rubbish, don't you?' Beth rolled her eyes as she started to undress Beatrix. 'I mean, you're supposed to have been seen holding hands with some guy and that's why you ditched Martin, because you're having an affair. As if!'

'I know. It's crazy, isn't it?' Polly sighed. 'People see something and get the completely wrong idea.'

'So you were holding hands with someone!' Beth exclaimed.

'Not exactly. I was checking his pulse, to be precise.' She quickly explained about the accident and what had happened later.

Beth chuckled. 'It's typical that Maureen should add two and two and come up with a hundred. Not that it will worry her, mind you. She's having far too much fun telling everyone what she thought she saw!'

'Don't I know it? It's amazing how fast news travels. I was at a couple of the outlying farms this morning and even they had heard all about my supposed exploits. I tell you, Beth, I'm sick and tired of being seen as some sort of *scarlet* woman!'

'You must be,' Beth said sympathetically. 'I know how hard it is when folk start gossiping about you. I've had my share, I can tell you, since Beatrix was born.'

'Really!' Polly exclaimed in surprise.

'Oh, yes. There's been speculation about who's this little one's daddy.' Beth shrugged. 'I suppose it's understandable in a way because Callum's not been seen around here for such a long time. I've just ignored it as there is no way I'm telling everyone that Beatrix was conceived the night he went away. That's my business and nobody else's.'

'I wish I could do the same but it isn't that simple.' Polly sighed when Beth looked at her. 'The man I'm supposed to be having an affair with is none too happy about what's being said. He has a son, you see, and he's worried that Joseph will hear the gossip and get the wrong idea.'

'Hmm, tricky. I don't know what to suggest, to be honest. If you kick up a fuss then people will only think there's some truth to the rumours. The old "the lady doth protest too much" scenario,' Beth added wryly, making quotation marks with her fingers.

'Exactly. I tried explaining that to Elliot but he wouldn't have it. He's not at all happy about being dragged into this.'

'You don't mean Elliot Grey, do you?' Beth whistled when Polly nodded. 'That must be awkward. Oh, I know you don't have a lot of contact with the hospital but you're in the same field so you're bound to come across him from time to time.'

'And he isn't happy about that either. If Elliot had his way then he would ban all community midwives, it seems,' Polly declared hotly. She took a deep breath when she saw the surprise on Beth's face. She didn't want her friend to guess how much it hurt to know how determined Elliot was to keep her out of every aspect of his life. 'Anyway, I'm sure it will all work out in the end once people find something else to talk about.'

'I'm sure it will. I just wish you didn't have to put up with this on top of everything else,' Beth said sympathetically. 'Calling off the wedding couldn't have been an easy decision for you and Martin. It took guts, in my opinion.'

'It wasn't easy but it was the right thing to do in the circumstances.' Polly sighed. 'I only wish that it hadn't happened at the very last moment and upset so many people.'

'Had you been having doubts for a while then?' Beth asked quietly.

'No, not at all.' Polly sighed. 'Marrying Martin was what I'd wanted for a long time.'

'Because being married to Martin would give you a sense of security,' Beth suggested astutely. 'You'd officially become part of his family.'

'I suppose so.' Polly frowned. Had that been a major factor in her decision to marry Martin? Although his parents had been appointed by the courts as their guardians, they had never adopted her and Peter. However, once she and Martin were married there would have been a proper family link. With the benefit of hindsight, Polly could see how appealing that idea had been and it was a shock to realise it.

'Losing your parents at such a young age must have been very difficult for you,' Beth continued quietly. 'After living with Martin's parents for all those years, it's understandable if you wanted to make sure that you would always be part of their family.'

'You're right, although I've never actually thought about it before,' Polly admitted. 'It just seemed the natural thing to do when

Martin and I started dating after I came back from university.'

'I can understand why you felt that way,' Beth assured her. 'But was it really enough to base a lifetime's commitment on? Are you sure you really loved him?'

'I thought I did,' Polly said slowly, her head reeling. Had she loved Martin, *really* loved him as the man she wanted to spend her life with? Or had her feelings been based on familiarity and a desire for security?

'I think that's your answer.' Beth smiled wryly when Polly looked at her. 'Oh, I know it didn't work out for me and Callum but we were in love at one time. I remember how it felt and you'd have known if you felt like that. You and Martin made the right decision when you called off your wedding.'

'It appears that we did, although it wasn't a joint decision as we've told everyone. It was Martin who called it off.' She grimaced. 'He's met someone else and wants to be with her. That's why he didn't want to marry me.'

'What?' Beth gaped at her. 'Martin's been having an affair?'

'Yes. He left me a letter, explaining that he couldn't marry me as he's in love with someone else. He suggested it might make it easier if I told everyone it was a mutual decision to cancel the wedding, although I'm starting to wonder if it was a mistake. The gossip couldn't be any worse if everyone knew I'd been jilted!'

'I don't know what to say!' Beth exclaimed. 'However, it seems a bit rich that the whole of Beesdale thinks you're the one who's been having a fling when it was Martin.'

'It's over and done with now, so it's probably best to leave things how they are. It will only start folk gossiping even more if they find out the truth at this stage and that's the last thing I want, quite frankly.'

'I suppose so, although I still don't think it's fair that you're being blamed for something you didn't do,' Beth declared.

'Maybe not, but I don't think I can claim to be totally blameless.' She sighed. 'Martin must have sensed that my reasons for marrying him weren't purely out of love, so it's understandable if he met someone else and fell for her. Anyway, enough about me. How's this little lady doing, apart from waking her poor mum at such an unearthly hour?'

Beth took the hint and changed the subject,

although Polly could tell that her friend was still upset about her carrying all the blame. It was good to have someone else on her side apart from Elliot, if he really was on her side and there was no guarantee of that after the way they had parted. She sighed softly as she saw Beth out. Elliot had been so gentle and caring as he had consoled her and it made the sudden switch back to his normal self all the more difficult to accept. He was so wary of showing his true feelings and she couldn't see that changing in the foreseeable future. The thought of him choosing to live such a lonely life hurt, especially after the glimpse she'd had of the real man beneath the veneer of aloofness. Elliot deserved so much more; he deserved to be loved and to love too. However, she doubted if he would agree with her. He preferred his lonely life to taking risks and there was little she could do to convince him otherwise.

Polly called in her next mum, determined not to think about him any more. Once she left Beesdale, Elliot would be just a memory. The trouble was that deep down she knew it wasn't that simple. Even if she never saw him again, it didn't mean that she would forget him.

\* \* \*

The week came to an end and the weekend rolled around. Elliot wasn't on call so he decided to take Joseph out for the day. He put together a picnic and stowed it in the car then loaded the lightweight wheelchair Joseph used for outings. The chair he used the rest of the time was too heavy to lift in and out of the car, so he had to make do with this pared-down version. Although he could walk short distances, he soon tired, and Elliot always took the chair along in case he needed it. It was second nature to cover all the bases, but he found himself wondering all of a sudden how anyone else would cope. Would they be happy to make all these preparations or would they find it became tedious after a while? How would Polly fare, for instance?

Elliot sighed as he went to fetch Joseph. It didn't matter how many times he told himself that Polly wasn't going to feature in his life because he still kept thinking about her. She had infiltrated his mind, the same as she had infiltrated his senses the other night. The minute he had touched her, he had been overwhelmed by feelings he couldn't control and he found it hard to accept that he was so weak-willed. He had to find a way to get back to normal, but so far he had failed to do so. It was as though Polly had taken him over, lock, stock and barrel, and there wasn't a thing he could do about it.

Saturday turned out to be a beautiful day with only a few fluffy white clouds drifting across the azure blue sky. Polly had a list of jobs that needed doing but she felt too restless to spend the day indoors. She ate her breakfast outside, seated at the tiny metal table on the equally tiny patio. Primrose Cottage was one of four which were used as holiday lets during the summer season and stood empty the rest of the year. They all looked neglected and in need of sprucing up. Polly knew that if she'd been planning to stay she would have had to make a lot of improvements, but it wasn't worth it for the length of time she hoped to be there. She had already received a letter inviting her for an interview in Cumbria at the end of the month and, although there was no guarantee she would be offered the post, she knew she stood a very good chance with her experience.

She sighed as she spread honey on a slice

of toast. Although she would miss Beesdale, it was becoming increasingly difficult as the rumours about her spread. She was tired of being blamed for something she hadn't done. The only thing that kept her going was the thought that in a few weeks' time she would be able to put it all behind her. Just for a moment an image of Elliot came to mind before she blanked it out. She wasn't going to change her mind about leaving for any reason. Or anyone.

Elliot drove to Beesdale Falls and parked in the car park. There were several other cars already there so he chose a space that gave him room to lift Joseph's chair out of the boot. Joseph was bubbling over with excitement at the thought of the outing and Elliot realised all of a sudden how long it had been since they had done anything fun like this together. Between the move from London and starting a new job, his time had been eaten up, and he resolved not to let it happen again. Spending time with Joseph was his number one priority from now on.

Joseph insisted on walking part of the way, only using his chair when the path became too rough for him to negotiate it safely. Elliot was breathing heavily by the time they reached the waterfall because it was tough pushing the chair over all the ruts, but it was worth it. Joseph was enthralled by the sight of the water tumbling into the gorge. He had brought his sketch pad along and wanted to draw a picture so Elliot sat down on the grass while he got his breath back.

The noise of the water rushing over the rocks was deafening so he didn't hear anyone approaching. It was only when a shadow fell over them that he looked up and felt his heart lurch when he saw Polly standing behind him. It was obvious from the surprise on her face that she'd had no idea he would be there. He also had the distinct impression that she wasn't pleased to see him either and the thought stung. He'd wasted hours thinking about her yet she didn't give a damn about him or the effect she'd had on his life!

Polly's heart sank to somewhere around the level of her feet. If she'd had any idea that Elliot would be there then she would never have come. She half turned to leave but just at that moment Joseph spotted her.

'Polly! Dad didn't tell me you were coming as well.'

'I…um…he didn't know,' she explained, avoiding looking at Elliot. That he wouldn't want her there was a given and she didn't need it ramming home to her. The thought was incredibly painful and she hurried on. 'I only decided this morning after breakfast that I felt like a day out.'

'So did Dad.' Joseph beamed at her. 'We've brought a picnic with us so you can share it now—can't she, Dad?'

'Oh, no,' Polly began at the same moment as Elliot spoke.

'I'm sure Polly has more important things to do than spend the day with us, Joseph.'

Polly felt annoyance run through her when she heard the warning in his voice. Did he honestly think that she hadn't worked it out for herself that he didn't want her spending time with them? Maybe it was the result of the week she'd had, all the whispered remarks, the sidelong glances, but she was tired of being treated like a pariah when she had done nothing to deserve it.

'Actually, I don't have anything more important to do, as it happens.' She smiled sweetly, seeing the annoyance in Elliot's eyes, but it was hard luck. He should never have started this if he wasn't prepared to face the consequences. 'I'd love to share your picnic, Joseph. Thank you.'

Elliot spread the rug on the ground, trying not to think about the last time he had used it, the day he had met Polly. It was only a few weeks ago yet it felt much longer than that. It was as though his life had been divided into two halves, before and after meeting Polly, and he didn't like the idea one little bit. He had been perfectly happy before he had met her... Hadn't he?

He frowned as he got up and headed back down the path to collect the cool box from the car. It was unsettling to find himself questioning what he had taken for granted before. Maybe he had decided to relocate to a different part of the country but his reasons for doing so had had nothing to do with him. He had made the decision so he could give Joseph a better quality of life—or so he had thought.

Was it true? he wondered suddenly. Had his decision to leave London been based solely on Joseph's needs? Or had there been another reason, one he hadn't examined too closely? Although he had enjoyed his job there, he had to admit that the constant pressure of dealing with the most vulnerable patients had started to get to him. Working in such a busy city as London had meant that his workload had been unrelenting, one tiny scrap of humanity after another requiring his skills. Although he had saved so many babies, far more than his peers if the statistics were to be believed, there had been many others he hadn't been able to help. Not even the most skilful surgeon could save every single patient he treated and each time he had failed, it had left its mark on him. Although he had buried his feelings beneath a veneer of professional detachment, he had felt for them, he realised, felt a deep sense of sorrow for all those children who would never grow up to be adults, for all the parents whose dreams had been shattered.

He had been there himself, been through the agony of wondering if his child would survive, but he'd been one of the lucky ones—his son had lived. However, each time he had lost one of those precious children, it had left a scar on his soul even if he had refused to admit it before. He might have pretended not to care but deep down he had, although it was only now that he was prepared to acknowledge it, now when his emotions had been unleashed since he had met Polly. She had been the catalyst even though he had no idea why. Hell and damnation, if he'd been told to choose a woman who would turn his life upside down then he couldn't have found anyone better than Polly. She had been jilted on her wedding day—she must have even more emotional baggage than him!

# CHAPTER EIGHT

POLLY COULD FEEL the waves of anger coming off Elliot and knew she was the reason for it. He was annoyed about her joining them for this picnic, she thought as she watched him arrange pieces of cooked chicken on a paper plate. Although his reaction seemed extreme to her mind, maybe she should make an effort to smooth things over. After all, she didn't want Joseph to think there was anything wrong when it would only upset him. She went over and knelt down on the rug, lowering her voice so that the child couldn't hear her.

'Look, I'm sorry if you have a problem with my being here. The last thing I want is to cause any trouble.'

'You should have thought of that before you agreed to join us,' Elliot said harshly, lifting a bottle of orange juice out of the cool box.

Polly bit back her sharp retort because it was obvious that Elliot wasn't interested in hearing her apology. He didn't want her there and that was it. It made her see that there was only one thing she could do in the circumstances. 'You're right; I should have done,' she said flatly. She glanced over at Joseph, who was busily colouring in his picture, oblivious to what was going on. It had been obvious how delighted he'd been to see her and it made her feel guilty all of a sudden. She didn't want him growing attached to her when she was leaving Beesdale in a few weeks' time. Maybe she had been trying to put Elliot in his place, but not at the expense of hurting his son.

'I'll make some excuse and get out of your way,' she said quietly as she turned back to Elliot.

'And that's your answer, is it? Run away and to hell with Joseph and the fact that he will be bitterly disappointed if you don't stay for the picnic?' He smiled grimly. 'Why am I not surprised? After all, why would you want to spend time with him when I'm sure you can find more exciting things to do?'

'That's not fair,' she protested then stopped

when a car drove into the car park and parked next to where they were sitting. A couple got out and started walking towards the waterfall. The young woman was heavily pregnant and Polly saw the man put his arm around her to help her over the rough ground. It was such a loving gesture that it brought a lump to Polly's throat. It brought it home to her that there was nobody who cared about her that much, nobody to help her if she needed it. She was completely on her own and whatever happened, good or bad, she would have to deal with it herself.

Polly felt her eyes fill with tears all of a sudden. She scrambled to her feet, not wanting to break down again in front of Elliot. Knowing him, he would probably think that she was doing it on purpose to gain his sympathy. She hurried over to her car, feeling more wretched than ever. Every time she did anything, it backfired on her. She'd thought she was doing the right thing by marrying Martin but look how that had turned out. And those stupid rumours would never have started if she hadn't tried to make sure that Elliot wasn't injured. It was as though she was jinxed!

'Wait! Don't go. Not like this, Polly.'

The urgency in Elliot's voice surprised her so much that she stopped. She turned around, her breath catching when she saw the expression on his face. Why was he looking at her as though he cared? He didn't care about her, as he had made it abundantly clear. The thought brought more tears to her eyes and she heard him sigh as he came over to her.

'I'm sorry, Polly. I never meant to upset you.'

'No?' She gave a broken little laugh. 'From where I'm standing I'd say it was precisely what you wanted to do.'

'Of course not.' He hesitated and she could tell that he was choosing his words with care. 'I just don't want you to upset Joseph. He's already growing very attached to you and I don't want him getting hurt.'

'I don't want him getting hurt either,' she said quietly.

Elliot sighed. 'I know you don't. It's just that I worry so much.'

'Because of the way his mother left him?' she suggested.

'Yes.' He grimaced. 'I suppose it was stupid of me to hope that Marianna would change her mind once he was born. After all, I knew to my cost how self-centred she was and having a child with a major handicap would have changed her life completely. But I still hoped that when she saw him she would feel differently.'

'Only she didn't.'

'No. She didn't even want to see him after he was born. I don't think she could face the thought of giving birth to a child who wasn't perfect.'

'So she's never seen him?' Polly asked, appalled.

'Once and that was only by accident when we bumped into her while we were out shopping.' He laughed bitterly. 'She couldn't wait to get away either.'

'How awful! Was Joseph upset?' she asked, her heart aching at the thought of the child suffering such a rejection.

'Very much so. He cried himself to sleep for several nights afterwards.' Elliot took a deep breath. 'That's why I can't risk him growing attached to anyone else, Polly. I don't want him getting hurt again. Even though I know you would never deliberately hurt him, you have enough to deal with right now, what with the wedding and everything else. That's why I feel it would be better if we didn't spend too much time together.'

'I understand,' she began then broke off when she heard someone shouting for help. The sound was coming from the direction of the waterfall and her heart sank as she recalled the young couple who had gone that way a short time earlier.

Elliot spun round. 'I'll go and see what's happened. Can you stay with Joseph?'

'Of course.' Polly hurried over to the little boy. Bending down, she gave him a hug when she saw the alarm on his face. 'Don't worry, sweetheart, your dad's gone to see what's happened. He won't be long.'

They waited for what seemed like ages. Polly was starting to get really worried as the minutes ticked past and there was no sign of Elliot. Was he all right or had something happened to him as well? She had visions of him diving into the river to rescue someone and getting swept away. In the end, she couldn't bear it any longer and took out her mobile phone so she could summon help. Her finger was actually hovering over the button when Elliot suddenly appeared. He wasn't alone; he had the young man she'd seen earlier with him and they were supporting the young woman between them. He looked over and beckoned to her.

'Can you lend a hand here, Polly? It looks like Sarah has gone into labour.'

'Good heavens!' Polly rushed over to them, smiling ruefully at the other woman. 'What a time for this to happen! Babies certainly choose their moment, don't they?'

Sarah dredged up a smile although Polly could tell how scared she was. 'This one certainly has. I'm not due for another couple of weeks, which is why Dave and I thought it would be all right if we had a day out. Everyone keeps telling me that first babies are always late so I never expected this to happen.'

'Well, there's nothing to worry about. We'll soon get you sorted out,' Polly assured her. 'It just so happens that I'm the local midwife, Polly Davies, and Elliot—Dr Grey—is in charge of the paediatric surgical unit at the local hospital.' She grinned at Sarah, wanting to reassure her. The last thing they needed was for Sarah to start panicking. 'You couldn't have chosen a better time and place to go into labour!'

* * *

'You're almost there. One more push should do it… Yes! That's it. Keep going.'

Elliot listened as Polly talked Sarah through the final stages of the delivery. The birth had been swift although none the less intense for that. Several times Sarah had shown signs of panic when the contractions had been very strong, but Polly had managed to keep her focused and he had to admit that he was impressed. It was clear that Polly was an excellent midwife and he found himself readjusting his opinion of the job she did. She was a professional through and through, yet she still had the gift of being able to connect with people. He could learn a lot from her.

The baby suddenly slid out into Polly's waiting hands and Elliot shook off the moment of introspection with a feeling of relief. His life had already changed thanks to Polly and he wasn't sure if he was ready to make any more adjustments just yet! He watched as Polly picked up a towel and started to rub the baby, feeling the first flicker of alarm run through him when he realised that the child still hadn't started crying. He could feel himself grow tense as he watched Polly gently flick her finger against the soles of the little boy's feet in an attempt to stimulate him to breathe, but it had no effect.

'What's wrong?' Sarah demanded shrilly. 'Why isn't he crying?'

'Just give me a second,' Polly murmured, quickly turning the baby over and patting his back. She looked up and Elliot could see the concern on her face when the baby still failed to take a breath. 'We need to clear his airway.'

'Right.'

Elliot didn't need to hear any more as he took a length of narrow tubing from the birthing kit and deftly inserted it into the baby's mouth while Polly held him. It took only seconds to draw off the mucus but he was very conscious of the time ticking past. Without access to any proper ventilating equipment, the baby wouldn't stand a chance if this didn't work. He held his breath as Polly laid the baby face down again and patted his back, but there was still no response. Reaching out, Elliot took him from her, fitting his mouth over the child's nose and mouth while he blew gently into his lungs. Every second that passed made the situation even more critical. The baby suddenly took a gasping breath and Elliot smiled in relief when the infant let out a loud wail as soon as he removed his mouth.

'Well, there doesn't seem to be much wrong with his lungs,' he observed, handing the squalling infant to Polly so she could clamp the cord and wrap him in the towel.

'Thank you so much,' Dave mumbled when Polly passed the baby to him. Tears were streaming down both parents' faces now and Elliot felt a lump come to his throat. Their relief was palpable and he couldn't help being affected by it.

He stood up, using the excuse that he needed to check on Joseph to make his escape. He hadn't felt like this for years, his emotions bubbling up and spilling over, and it scared him to realise how little control he had. He had felt like this when he had met Marianna and it had been all that emotion that had led him to marry her. Would he have done so if he'd been thinking clearly? Would he have ignored all the warning signs that she wasn't the sweetly innocent woman she pretended to be? Of course he wouldn't! He would have let things run their course, enjoyed spending time with her, enjoyed *sleeping* with her, but he would never have married her. He had allowed his feelings to skew his judgement and he had paid the price for it too.

Elliot felt a wave of pain wash over him as he looked back at Polly. He wouldn't make the same mistake again because it wasn't only him who could get hurt this time. Joseph would be devastated if he grew to love Polly and she let him down. It was a risk Elliot wasn't prepared to take and *that* was why he couldn't allow Polly into his life, no matter how much he longed to do so.

The ambulance arrived about half an hour later. By that time Polly had delivered the placenta and got Sarah tidied up. Joseph had come to see the baby and he was fascinated by the sight of the tiny infant.

'Was I that little when I was born?' he asked Elliot.

'Yes, you were, although it's a normal size for a newborn baby,' Elliot explained quietly.

Polly sighed when she heard the emotion in his voice. Was he thinking about how different Joseph's arrival into the world had been? she wondered sadly. Although there'd been that hiccup when Sarah's baby had failed to breathe initially, he was perfect in every respect. Elliot wouldn't be human if he didn't compare him to how Joseph must have looked when he'd been born. The thought brought a lump to her throat and she busied herself with helping Sarah into the ambulance. Elliot wouldn't appreciate it if she tried to comfort him.

'Thank you so much. I don't know what would have happened if you and Dr Grey hadn't been here—' Sarah broke off, shuddering at the thought.

'But we were here so don't think about it.' Polly squeezed her hand. 'Just concentrate on enjoying that gorgeous little boy of yours.'

'I will.' Sarah looked at Joseph and bit her lip. 'It makes me realise just how lucky we are.'

Polly didn't say anything. To an outsider it must seem as though Joseph's disability was a huge drawback but, having spent time with him, she knew that wasn't the case at all. He was such a plucky little boy that one soon forgot that he was different from other children.

She had a final word with the paramedics to make sure they knew that the baby had had a problem breathing initially then stood aside while the ambulance drove out of the car park. Although Sarah was booked into a hospital close to where she lived, she would be taken to their local hospital and stay there for the next twenty-four hours at least. It might not be what she had planned but she and the baby were both safe and well and that was what mattered most of all.

'That's that then.'

She looked round when Elliot spoke, feeling all sorts of emotions churning inside her. He had been the consummate professional while they had dealt with Sarah's baby, but she could tell that what had happened had affected him. However, typically, he was hiding his feelings.

'So it seems,' Polly said, wishing she could make him understand what a mistake it was. Bottling up his feelings wouldn't do him any good; he needed to face up to them and admit that he cared, but there seemed very little chance of that happening. 'At least everything worked out in the end,' she said, trying not to dwell on that thought. 'There was a moment when I was afraid we weren't going to be able to start the baby breathing.'

'So was I, which is why I think it's a mistake to allow a woman to give birth at home,' he said curtly. 'All right, so what happened today couldn't have been foreseen, but the same situation could have occurred during a home birth. That's why home births should be banned.'

His tone was confrontational and Polly frowned. She had a feeling that he was being deliberately provocative, but why? Because it was easier than admitting how relieved he'd been when Sarah's baby had taken his first breath? It was on the tip of her tongue to say something and force him to admit it when Joseph interrupted them.

'Are we going to have our picnic now, Dad?'

'I think it's a bit too late to have it now.' Elliot glanced at the sky, which had become very overcast. 'It looks like it's going to rain so why don't we pack everything up and take it home? I'll put the rug on the sitting room floor and we can have our picnic in there instead.'

'Cool!' Joseph exclaimed. He turned excitedly to Polly. 'It'll be fun, won't it?'

'Oh…erm…I'm not sure if I can come,' she said hurriedly.

'But you have to!'

Joseph sounded really upset and she sighed. Although she hated to disappoint him, she wasn't sure if it would be wise to prolong the afternoon after what Elliot had told her earlier. The last thing she wanted was Joseph growing attached to her when she would be leaving Beesdale. He had already suffered the heartache of having his mother abandon him and, while she didn't consider herself to be in that category, it could upset him if she left him as well. Difficult though it was, she knew there was only one thing she could do.

'I'm sorry, Joseph, but I have things to do,' she explained, feeling awful when his face fell.

'Can't you do them and *then* come to the picnic?' he pleaded. 'We can wait for you, can't we, Dad?'

'Polly has just explained that she can't come,' Elliot said firmly. He glanced at her and she knew that she'd made the right decision when she saw the relief in his eyes. 'You can't expect her to spend the whole day with us when she has things to do.'

'What sort of things?' Joseph demanded.

'First of all I need to re-pack my bag in case I get called out. Then I'll have to write a report about what happened this afternoon and email it to the hospital as well as send a copy to the senior midwife who supervises this area,' she explained, dredging up reasons because it was what she needed to do. 'Much as I'd love to come, Joseph, I'll have to miss your picnic, I'm afraid.'

'Then maybe you can come for tea next week instead,' Joseph said quickly. He turned to Elliot. 'Polly can come on Saturday when I'm not at school, can't she?'

'That's up to Polly. She may have already made plans for the weekend,' Elliot replied evenly, but Polly could tell that he wasn't happy about the idea. She wasn't happy about it either, although it was hard to come up with an excuse when she had been put on the spot like that.

'I may have to work next weekend,' she said, fudging the truth. Although she had agreed to provide cover for a neighbouring area, she wasn't actually rostered to work.

'But you'll come if you can?' Joseph insisted.

'I suppose so,' she agreed reluctantly.

'Promise?' Joseph demanded and she sighed. He wasn't going to give up easily, just like his father, in fact. Once Elliot got an idea into his head, like the dangers of home births, for instance, then it would take a miracle to shift it!

'Promise,' she said because it was easier than trying to put Joseph off.

'Now you *have* to come,' Joseph declared. 'Once you've made a promise then you can't break it. Can you, Dad?'

'No, you can't, although not everyone understands that, unfortunately.'

Polly shivered when she heard the bitterness in his voice. Was Elliot thinking about the promises his ex-wife had made when they had married? She knew it was true and it hurt to know how he must have suffered. The fact that he had hoped she would change her mind once Joseph was born was an indication of how much he must have loved her. Did he still love her? she wondered. Bearing in mind that he kept a photograph of her in his study, it appeared that he did and for some reason it made it even more painful to know that, after all this time and everything she had done, he still hadn't got over her. She bit her lip as she was forced to face the truth. He probably never would get over her.

# CHAPTER NINE

ELLIOT DECIDED TO visit Sarah and her baby when he went into work the following Monday. He had already phoned the maternity unit to check on them and had been informed that they were being kept in as the baby had developed jaundice. A lot of babies developed jaundice in the days following their birth. It was usually the result of an immature liver failing to excrete bilirubin—a bile pigment—efficiently and it would clear up by the end of the first week. Treatment consisted of extra fluids along with phototherapy. Occasionally, the condition was caused by something more serious but Elliot was hoping that wasn't the case in this instance. Strangely enough, he felt a sense of connection to this baby. Having played such a large part in his birth, he felt personally involved and it surprised him. It wasn't usual for him to feel like this, so what was different this time? Was it the fact that he and Polly had worked together to bring this child into the world?

He sighed as he keyed in the security code and let himself into the maternity unit. Everything came back to Polly, didn't it? Everything he did or felt seemed to start with her and it was hard to accept that he was no longer the self-sufficient person he had been before. Making it clear that he didn't want her spending time with him and Joseph should help, but he had a feeling that it wasn't the cure he hoped it would be. Not seeing Polly was one thing. Not thinking about her was something entirely different!

It was hard to ignore that thought as he stopped at the desk and had a word with the sister. It appeared that Sarah's baby had a mild form of jaundice, which was good news. He checked which room Sarah was in and tapped on the door, summoning a smile before he went in. What had Polly said once, something about him working on his people skills? Maybe he should get some practice, although it was slightly galling to know that once again she was influencing his behaviour.

'Dr Grey! I didn't know you were coming

to see us.' Sarah beamed up at him. 'Is Polly with you?'

'I'm afraid not,' Elliot replied, gritting his teeth because once again Polly had made her presence felt.

'Oh, that's a shame.' Sarah looked crestfallen for a moment before she rallied. 'Still, at least you're here so you can give her this, can't you?' She handed him a sparkly gold carrier bag. 'It's just some chocolates to say thank you for everything she did on Saturday. I wouldn't have got through it if Polly hadn't been there. She was brilliant!'

'I'm sure she will appreciate them,' Elliot said, trying to inject a note of enthusiasm into his voice. However, the thought of being responsible for passing on the gift made him feel all churned up inside. He was trying to avoid Polly, not finding more reasons to see her.

'I hope so.' Sarah smiled at him. 'I envy the mums who have her to deliver their babies. Oh, the staff at my local maternity unit are nice enough but I never really got to know them. Each time I went for a check-up, I saw someone different so there was never a chance to form a bond with any of them.'

'No, I can see that,' Elliot replied slowly. 'Does it really matter that much, though? Surely the most important thing is to know that your baby will be safe when it's born?'

'Of course, but being able to relate to the midwife—like I did to Polly—makes a huge difference. I'd have been totally stressed out if it weren't for her, especially when Matthew didn't start breathing at first. But I knew she'd help him—that you both would,' Sarah added hastily. 'You were great too, Dr Grey. I'm very grateful for all you did as well.'

'I was pleased to help,' Elliot replied truthfully. He spent a few more minutes with Sarah then left, stopping at the nursery on his way out to see baby Matthew. He was in a special crib used for phototherapy treatment and looked quite content.

Elliot made his way to his office, thinking about what Sarah had said. Even though she had been through all the trauma surrounding Matthew's birth, she didn't appear to think it would have been better if she'd had him in hospital. On the contrary, she envied the mums who were cared for at home by Polly. Had he been wrong to take such a hard stance when it came to home births? he wondered suddenly. Was he so biased by all the damaged babies he had treated over the years that he had refused to consider the advantages? Everyone knew that mothers did far better if they felt confident during the birth and Polly was wonderful at making them feel they could cope. She also related to them as people and not just as patients and that, too, must make it easier for them. Adding it all up, maybe there was a place for home births after all?

It was the first time he had questioned his beliefs on the subject and it was unsettling to wonder if he had failed to see the bigger picture. Elliot sighed as he booted up the computer to check his Theatre list. He had done nothing but question himself ever since he had arrived in Beesdale and it was all down to one woman. Polly was responsible for an awful lot of soul-searching!

Polly was exhausted by the time she got home just after seven that night. She'd been called out in the early hours of the morning to Barnsthwaite Farm after Anna Barnsthwaite had gone into labour. Although it was Anna's second child, it had been a long and gruelling birth, not made any easier by the fact that Anna's mother-in-law had been there looking after her three-year-old granddaughter. Every time Polly had left the room to fetch something, Mrs Barnsthwaite had been there, staring at her. It had got to the point where she'd felt that she had to say something but, thankfully, the baby had made her appearance then and she had let it pass. However, if that was an example of what she would have to put up with then she couldn't wait to leave. Even starting afresh, with all its attendant problems, would be better than that.

She let herself into the cottage, hoping that a cup of tea would help to revive her. There was another mum due to give birth any day and she only hoped the baby wouldn't choose that night to make its appearance. Closing the front door, she headed to the kitchen then realised all of a sudden that the hall floor was ankle-deep in water. Leaving her bag on the stairs, she paddled through it, her heart sinking as she took in the scene that met her. Water was pouring through the ceiling, obviously coming from the bathroom above. The force of the water had brought down a large section of the ceiling and there were pieces of plasterboard all over the place. The kettle was ruined and the toaster and she didn't dare touch the electric stove because it was covered with water. The place was a wreck and she had no idea what to do first.

In the end, she paddled back along the hall and switched off the electricity. Now she had no power either but it was safer than leaving it on and getting electrocuted. Taking her phone out of her bag, she rang the letting agents but the office was closed for the night. She left a brief message and hung up, wondering where to find the stopcock so she could turn off the water. Whether she would be able to spend the night in the cottage very much depended on the state of the bedroom, but she would check that after she had seen to the water.

Polly paddled back to the kitchen and found the stopcock under the sink. It was stiff from lack of use and resisted her attempts to turn it. Resting her forehead against the sink, she groaned. She really didn't need this on top of the day she'd had! When there was a knock on the front door she scrambled to her feet, praying that the letting agent had somehow got her message. Hopefully, he could find a plumber and get this sorted out. She hurried along the hall and flung open the door.

'Thank heavens!' she began then stopped when she realised that it wasn't the agent but Elliot who was standing on the step. He was holding a sparkly gold gift bag and he went to hand it to her when all of a sudden there was an almighty crash and a wave of water swept down the hall, soaking them both.

'What in heaven's name is going on?' he demanded, glaring down at his wet trousers.

'There's been a leak and I can't turn the water off,' Polly explained shortly because she didn't appreciate being made to feel that it was her fault he'd got a soaking.

'Show me where it is,' he ordered, stepping inside.

Polly debated telling him that she could manage, only it was blatantly obvious that she couldn't. She led him down the hall, groaning under her breath when she saw the state of the kitchen. It had been bad enough before but now the water tank had fallen through the ceiling, completely demolishing it. Water was gushing out of the broken pipes, forming an indoor waterfall over the sink. 'The stopcock's under there,' she muttered, pointing to the cupboard.

'It would be,' Elliot said as he paddled over to the sink. Water cascaded over him as he crouched down and grasped hold of the tap. It took several attempts before he managed to turn it and by that time he was soaked to the skin.

Polly stared around at the chaos that surrounded them. Everything was ruined—the dishes smashed, the fridge floating, most of the ceiling on the floor. There was no way that she could stay in the cottage tonight but where could she go? Try as she might, she couldn't come up with anywhere and it was the final straw. Tears began to pour down her face. She had never felt so completely alone in her entire life.

Elliot felt his insides twist when he saw the tears streaming down Polly's face. Even though he didn't want to get involved, he couldn't ignore what was happening. Stepping forward, he drew her into his arms and held her. He could feel her shaking as sobs racked her body and his insides twisted that bit more. It didn't seem fair that she had to contend with this on top of everything else.

He ran his hand down her back in an attempt to comfort her. Her clothes were soaking wet and he could feel the heat of her skin beneath his palm as he followed the line of her spine until he came to the hollow just above her bottom and paused. He knew that he should stop there and not go any further. After all, he was trying to console her, not seduce her, yet the temptation to go that bit further was too hard to resist. His hand moved on, gliding over the shapely curve of her bottom as he felt his breath catch. A lot of the women he had known had been rail-thin, starving themselves to conform to today's view of feminine beauty, but not Polly. She had curves in all the right places, curves he ached to explore.

He drew her closer as he let his fingers begin the return journey. His clothes were soaking as well and he could feel her body imprinting itself on his. Heat flowed through him when he felt her breasts pressing against his chest, felt her nipples harden as they brushed against him. He must have made some sort of a sound because her eyes rose to his and he could see the shock they held, along with something else, something that made his heart race. Polly wanted him and there was no way that she could hide how she felt, no way that he couldn't respond to it either.

His head dipped until his mouth was just a hair's breadth away from hers. He could taste the sweetness of her breath on his lips and he shuddered. He had kissed a lot of women over the years but he had never felt this sense of excitement and anticipation that he felt right now. Kissing Polly was something he had never planned on doing. After the last time, when it had so nearly happened, he had sworn he would never put himself in this position again. And yet the thought of kissing her aroused him in a way nothing else had done in years. He knew that he *had* to kiss her. It was as vital to him as breathing!

His head lowered until his mouth came to rest against hers and he groaned when he felt a host of sensations hit him. Heat and softness, sweetness and pleasure—it was hard to know which came first, not that it mattered. The only thing that mattered was the fact that his lips were on hers. In that second, Elliot realised just how much he had longed to do this. Oh, he might have sworn it would never happen but, deep down, he had hoped that it would. He needed this kiss so much—needed it to make sense of everything that had happened lately, all those doubts he'd had, this constant desire to examine his actions. Kissing Polly would prove one way or the other what he was too afraid to admit—that he cared about her. Cared deeply.

Polly could feel the blood racing through her veins when Elliot's mouth settled on hers. His lips felt so cool at first and yet, beneath the chill, she could sense their heat. That he wanted her was obvious, just as it was obvious that she wanted him, but was it right to allow desire to sweep them away and make them forget all the reasons why this shouldn't happen? Maybe she did want him to kiss her, but how would she feel after it was over? How would *he* feel when he realised what he had done? Neither of them was thinking clearly at this moment but that would change: it was bound to. She couldn't bear to think that he would regret this kiss, wish it hadn't happened, blame *her* because it had. For this kiss to mean anything it had to be regret free, and it could never be that. Elliot wouldn't let it.

Polly's heart was aching as she stepped back. Elliot didn't say a word but she saw the way his face closed up and guilt overwhelmed her. Should she explain that she wasn't rejecting him? That she was only trying to spare him even more heartache? She wanted to but she knew that he wouldn't want to listen. Not now. Not when his emotions were so raw. Not when he was hurting, as she was hurting too.

'It's obvious that you can't stay here tonight. You'd better pack a bag.'

Polly flinched when she heard the chill in his voice, but what had she expected? That he would speak to her lovingly, caringly after she had rejected him? It was hard to find the right note, hard to batten down the need to explain why she had done what she had. Maybe later she would find the right moment, but not now.

'It's probably not as bad as it looks,' she began, but he didn't let her finish.

'No, it's worse.' He glanced at the gaping hole in the ceiling then looked back at her. 'There's no way you can stay here. You've no electricity or water—well, no clean water, anyway. Go and pack a bag and let's get out of here.'

'But I've nowhere to go!' she protested, hurt almost beyond bearing by the ice in his voice. 'I can hardly turn up on someone's doorstep at this time and ask if I can stay the night.'

'I'm sure your friends would happily offer you a bed, but there's no need to bother them because you're coming home with me.' He strode to the door, pausing when he realised that she hadn't moved. 'What are you waiting for? I have to get back for Joseph so go and pack what you need. I'll be outside in the car.'

'Are you sure it's a good idea?' Polly said softly.

He smiled thinly, although there was no trace of amusement in his eyes. 'If you're worried that I am going to chance my luck again then don't be. I'm not that stupid.'

Polly took a deep breath after he left but it did nothing to ease the pain. She had been trying to spare him any more heartache but it had misfired horribly. Elliot thought that she hadn't wanted him to kiss her and it was so far from the truth that it would have been laughable if it weren't so tragic. She had wanted that kiss with every fibre of her being, wanted it more than she had wanted anything in her entire life, and it was a revelation to realise it.

Polly went upstairs and packed some clothes into a case, her heart racing. Beth had said that she would have known if she'd been in love and Beth had been right too. She hadn't been in love with Martin. She had loved him as a friend, as someone who could offer her the security she longed for, but that was all. She could see that now, could see that it was why she hadn't been completely devastated when he had called off their wedding. Oh, she had been hurt and angry, humiliated too, but it hadn't felt as though her world had ended, had it?

Picking up the case, Polly made her way downstairs. Elliot was waiting in his car. He got out when he saw her and took the case off her. Polly thanked him politely as she slid into the passenger seat and he nodded as he got behind the wheel, although he didn't say anything. Maybe he thought there was nothing left to say but she knew there was. There was so much that it seemed to be bubbling inside her head like a boiling cauldron. She wanted to explain why she had stopped him kissing her, plead with him to forgive her, beg him to kiss her again, but how could she? How could she entreat him to do something she knew in her heart he would regret?

It was why she had stopped him kissing her in the first place and nothing had changed. Not really. Not for him. The fact that she had realised she was falling in love with him would make no difference to him. It wouldn't alter the fact that he was still in love with his ex-wife, still scarred by her leaving him. All it would do was give him another reason to lock away his emotions, and that was the last thing she wanted. She wanted him to be happy, to build a new life here for himself and Joseph. Maybe it would take time but he had made a start and, once he grew more comfortable about admitting that he had feelings, it would get easier. He would be able to move on and leave the past behind him, maybe even consider having another relationship in time.

Polly took a deep breath because the truth had to be faced. She wouldn't be the one Elliot turned to if and when he was ready to start a new relationship. She would have left Beesdale by then and she would be simply part of his past.

Joseph was still up when they got back to the house. Elliot carried Polly's case inside, mentally gearing himself up for the onslaught he knew would follow as soon as his son saw Polly. Normally, he loved Joseph's full-on approach to life, the fact that the child wanted to know the ins and outs of everything that happened, but tonight he could have done without it. Done without the questions, done without the answers. He felt too raw to think clearly. Polly had rejected his kiss—rejected *him*. It shouldn't have mattered a jot but it did.

'Polly! What are you doing here?' Joseph came rushing along the hall in his wheelchair when he saw them. He glanced at the case Elliot was holding and his eyes widened. 'Are you staying the night with us?'

'I...um... Yes.'

Elliot frowned when he heard the catch in Polly's voice. They hadn't spoken on the drive over. There'd been nothing he had wanted to say and obviously Polly had felt the same. It surprised him to hear how upset she sounded now. Was it what had happened to the cottage, he wondered, the loss of her home and belongings? Or was it the aftermath of that kiss?

It was impossible to know without asking her and that was one question he definitely didn't intend to raise. He turned to Joseph, forcing a smile when he saw the curiosity on his face. 'Polly's cottage is flooded. A pipe must have burst and the water has brought down the kitchen ceiling. She couldn't stay there so she's going to spend the night with us.'

'Wow!' Joseph was agog to hear more but Elliot had no intention of discussing every little detail with him…

His heart lurched as once again he recalled that kiss. He'd thought Polly had been with him every step of the way; she had certainly given him that impression! How could he have been so wrong? Why hadn't he realised that it wasn't what she had wanted? Had he allowed his own desire to blind him to her feelings? Elliot tried to convince himself that it was the explanation but he didn't believe it. Not when he remembered the way she had looked at him. There had been genuine desire in her eyes, a hunger that had been all too real. So why had she called a halt? Why had she denied herself that kiss when she had wanted it as much as him?

It didn't make sense, or at least *he* couldn't make any sense of it. As he followed Joseph and Polly along the hall, Elliot tried his best to understand what had happened. Maybe he should have let it go, chalked it up to experience and tried to forget about it, but it was impossible when his heart was aching like this. It had hurt—hurt such a lot to be rejected—and, whilst he hated to admit it, he needed answers. If Polly had wanted him, why had she pushed him away?

# CHAPTER TEN

POLLY WAS AWAKE early the following morning. She had slept surprisingly well con-
sidering everything that had happened the
night before. She showered and dressed then
made her way downstairs, hesitating when
she found Elliot in the kitchen, nursing a cup
of coffee. He looked round when he heard her
footsteps and smiled, but she could tell the
effort it cost him and was overwhelmed by
guilt once more.

She had to explain about that kiss! There
had been no opportunity last night with Joseph there. Even after Joseph had gone to
bed the right moment simply hadn't presented
itself. Although Elliot had been unfailingly
polite as he had asked her if she'd wanted
something to eat, she had sensed his with-
drawal and refused. She had gone to bed a
short time later, still without having said any-

thing, but she couldn't carry on this way. It wasn't fair to let him go on thinking that she hadn't wanted him to kiss her, but how could she explain without him guessing the truth— that she was falling in love with him? She didn't want to burden him with that when he had so much else to deal with.

'You're up early,' he said, getting up to take another mug out of the cupboard. He held it aloft. 'Coffee?'

'Please.' Polly watched as he poured coffee into the mug. He was dressed for work although he wasn't wearing his suit jacket yet. The sight of his broad shoulders clearly outlined beneath the thin fabric of his shirt made a shaft of heat run through her. She had felt the power of his body for herself last night. Their clothes had been soaked through and she'd felt every muscle and sinew when he had held her in his arms. She longed to be back in them again, only without the barrier of clothing this time. She could imagine how warm and smooth his skin would feel…

'Here you go. Milk, no sugar, just how you like it.'

Polly jumped when he set the mug of coffee on the table in front of her. Her eyes flew to his and she knew that he could see every-thing she was feeling at that moment—all the desire, all the need... She dragged her gaze away and picked up the mug, her hand shak-ing as she lifted it to her lips. Would Elliot say something? Or would he opt to let it go rather than deal with any more complicated emotions?

'About last night, Polly, I need to ask you something.' His voice was calm, controlled, yet she sensed that he was anything but that underneath. This was important to him, vi-tally important, and she knew that she would have to tell him the truth even if he wouldn't want to hear it.

'Yes?' she whispered, her nerves so tightly strung that it felt as though she had shouted the word out loud.

'Why did you stop me kissing you?' He gave a self-deprecating laugh that brought a sudden lump to her throat. That he was pre-pared to open himself up this much to hear her answer was unbearably moving. 'Because I have to say that it felt as though you wanted it to happen as much as I did.'

'I did,' she said huskily. 'You were right, Elliot—I did want you to kiss me.'

'Then why did you stop me?' He covered her hand with his and his touch was so gentle that it brought tears to her eyes.

'I had to. I didn't want to, but I *had* to. I couldn't have lived with the guilt if I'd let you kiss me.' She broke off, needing a moment to find the right words to explain.

'I see. It makes perfect sense now. Stupid of me not to have realised it before.' He gave a harsh laugh that brought her eyes back to his face and she went cold when she saw the way he was looking at her. 'Despite the fact that your fiancé jilted you for someone else, you still feel a certain loyalty to him. Maybe you still love him and hope to win him back— who knows?' He pushed back his chair, his face as hard as stone as he looked down at her. 'I wish you luck, Polly, even though I think you're making a big mistake. Take it from someone who knows, once he's strayed then he'll do it again. I can guarantee it!'

'Elliot, no!' Polly shot to her feet, overturning the chair in her haste. 'It wasn't like that,' she began, but he shook his head.

'It doesn't matter. I've had my answer and that's all I wanted.' He looked round when the front door opened. 'Here's Mrs Danton so I'll get off. Don't worry about Joseph. She'll see to him. I hope you manage to find somewhere to live while the cottage is being repaired.'

Polly picked up the chair as he left the room. She heard him speaking to the house-keeper then the sound of the front door closing and that was it. He had gone, left before she'd had a chance to explain why she had felt guilty. Not because of Martin but because of how *he* would have felt if he had kissed her. How ironic that he had turned the truth on its head. She didn't know whether to laugh or cry and in the end she did neither. Elliot had his answer and even if it wasn't the right one, it would serve the same purpose. Now there was even more reason to stay out of his life and she would start by finding somewhere else to live. One thing was certain: Elliot didn't want her here.

In the end, Polly asked Beth if she could stay with her. She had contacted the letting agents and they had agreed to speak to the owners of the cottage and ask them if she could move into one of the other cottages while the repairs were being done. Apparently the owners travelled abroad a lot and the agents had warned her that it could take some time to get in touch with them. Although she felt awful about having to ask her friend to put her up, she didn't have a choice. There were no other rental properties available in Beesdale or the surrounding area and she had to stay somewhere. Beth was typically welcoming and assured her that it was no trouble at all having her to stay. Polly was grateful, although she drew the line when Beth offered to move baby Bea's cot into her own bedroom so that Polly could put up the camp bed in the nursery.

'I'll be fine on the couch, Beth, really I will. I just need somewhere to sleep for a few nights until everything is sorted out.'

'It doesn't sound as though you'll be able to move back into the cottage for a while,' Beth pointed out. 'It will take weeks to do the repairs and get everything back in place.'

'I'm hoping that I can stay in one of the other cottages,' Polly explained. 'They're all empty and I can't see any reason why I can't move into one of them. I won't be here that long for it to make much difference.'

'Why? Where are you going?' Beth asked in surprise.

'I'm not sure yet.' Polly grimaced. 'I've handed in my notice and I have an interview in Cumbria at the end of the month so it may turn out that I move there.'

'You're not leaving because of all those stupid rumours, are you?' Beth said hotly. 'It's not right that a load of old biddies with nothing better to do are driving you away!'

'It's partly that,' Polly admitted. 'I hate the fact that everyone is talking about me. Then there's how difficult it's going to be if I stay here and keep bumping into Martin, as is bound to happen.'

'It shouldn't be you who's having to move away,' Beth said stoutly. 'Martin's the one who had an affair, not you.'

'Yes, but I can't expect him to leave when both his family and his work are here. It's not as though I have any family here, is it?' She sighed. 'Anyway, it isn't only that—there are other considerations.'

'Like Elliot Grey being dragged into this as the other man?' Beth frowned. 'Has he been kicking off about it again?'

'Not really, although he's not best pleased, as you'd expect. Anyhow, after what happened last night, it'll be a relief to put some distance between us.'

'Why? What happened?' Beth demanded.

'Elliot kissed me. And I made a complete and utter mess of everything.'

'He kissed you!'

'I…erm…yes,' Polly muttered, wishing she hadn't let her tongue run away with her. She bit her lip, forcing back the tears. She had to hold onto the thought that she had done the right thing, even if it didn't feel like it.

'I had no idea things had progressed so far,' Beth declared. She fixed Polly with gimlet eyes. 'And what do you mean—that you made a mess of everything? How do you mess up a kiss?'

'When you put a stop to it.' Polly sighed when she saw the incredulity on Beth's face. 'It wouldn't have been right to let him carry on kissing me when he would have regretted it.'

'I'm sure he's old enough to know what he was doing,' Beth said tartly.

'I suppose so. But I didn't want him to feel guilty about it.' She shook her head. 'I tried explaining that to him this morning but he got the completely wrong end of the stick and thought I was talking about Martin and that *I'd* have felt guilty if we'd carried on kissing.'

'And would you?' Beth asked.

'No. I...well, I realised that I was never in love with Martin. I certainly don't want to get back with him, as Elliot seems to think.'

'Poor you. It's a lot to take in.'

'What is?'

'Falling in love.' Beth gave her a hug. 'I'm right, aren't I?'

'Uh-huh,' Polly murmured, a single tear trickling down her cheek. She wiped her face on her sleeve when Beth let her go. 'I'm turning into a real Moaning Minnie, weeping and wailing all the time!'

'Best to get it out of your system is my advice.' Beth grinned at her. 'So how do you plan to put Elliot right about what happened? I take it that's what you're intending to do.'

'No. I doubt if he'd believe me even if I tried and there's no point anyway. He's still in love with his ex-wife even though she behaved appallingly, from what I can gather.'

'And has he told you that?'

'He didn't have to. It's patently clear how he feels about her.'

'And that's why you're leaving?' Beth said quietly.

'It's one of the reasons, yes. I...I don't want to stay here and keep hoping that Elliot will change his mind. It would be too hard.'

'It's your decision, obviously, but promise me that you'll think about what you're doing.' Beth sighed. 'It's far too easy to set yourself on a particular course and then live to regret it.'

Polly guessed that her friend was thinking about her relationship with Callum O'Neill, Beatrix's father. Although Beth had said very little about why they had split up, Polly knew it had been very traumatic for her, especially when Beth had found out that she was pregnant after Callum had left. Although Beth had written to him to tell him about the baby, he had never replied, and that must have made it so much worse. Beth must have been devastated, just like Elliot had been when Joseph's mother had left him.

Thankfully, they changed the subject but Polly couldn't shake off the feeling that she should have tried harder to explain her actions to Elliot. She couldn't bear to imagine him comparing her to his ex-wife. She was nothing like Joseph's mother, but would he believe that after the way she had seemingly rejected him last night? The thought stayed with her, nagging away at her at every stray moment. She didn't want Elliot to think that she was anything like the woman who had hurt him so badly.

# CHAPTER ELEVEN

ELLIOT FELT COMPLETELY drained when he arrived at work. He had spent a sleepless night, going over and over everything that had happened with Polly. He had kissed a lot of women in his time but he had never experienced that feeling of excitement and anticipation that he'd felt last night. Now all he felt was deflated. Polly might have felt the same as him but she had called a halt out of loyalty to her former fiancé. It hurt to know that she felt guilty about what had happened, and it hurt even more to know that she was still in love with the man who had jilted her. Couldn't she see what a mistake she was making? Didn't she understand that if had cheated on her once then he would do it again and again? Apparently not if she was hoping to win him back!

The thought sliced into him like a red-hot

knife. It was hard to respond when his secretary wished him a cheerful good morning as he went into his office. He was due in Theatre that morning and he brought up the list on the computer. There had been an admission the previous day, a child suffering from Hirschsprung's disease, a congenital condition which caused extreme constipation and intestinal blockage. Elliot decided to attend to that first as it also caused painful spasms and he didn't want the little girl to suffer any longer. He would concentrate on helping her and all the other children and forget about himself and what he wanted. He had everything he needed—a job he loved, a son he adored—and there was no excuse for wanting more, definitely no excuse for wanting Polly to share his life. He had been there, done that, torn up the T-shirt and sworn he wouldn't get involved again.

Marianna had shown him that love was a myth, something that only happened in fairy tales. He had been taken in by her apparent charm and her beauty but he had soon realised that it was all smoke and mirrors, not real. Her appeal had quickly faded and he'd been on the point of telling her that he wanted a divorce when she had announced that she was pregnant and any thoughts he'd had about them parting had been set aside. Would they have stayed together if Joseph had been born without a disability? Would they have worked through their differences and reached a compromise for the sake of their child?

He doubted it. He and Marianna had had nothing in common, nothing to form a solid basis for their relationship, and that was why it hadn't worked. It didn't mean that it would happen again if he met someone else, though, he thought suddenly, someone he could relate to like Polly. She was very different from his ex-wife: kind, caring, loving, faithful. Even this morning when she had explained about that kiss, she hadn't tried to lie or make excuses. She had told him the truth and even though it was painful to know that she was in love with another man, he valued her honesty. Sadness washed over him. Polly was the woman he could have loved if he'd only had the chance.

Polly was already awake when her phone rang shortly before six the following morning. She hurriedly answered it, not wanting to wake

Beth and the baby. It was Amy Carmichael, her voice shaking with fear as she told Polly that she was having pains. Although Amy wasn't due for another month, babies with a congenital diaphragmatic hernia often had an increased level of amniotic fluid around them which could lead to an early birth. Polly told Amy that she would be there as soon as she could and that she would phone for an ambulance as well as contact the hospital to warn them. If the baby was on his way then he would need support if he was to have any chance of surviving.

She hurriedly dressed, using the kitchen sink to wash her hands and splash water on her face as there was no time for a shower. Beth appeared as she was checking her case and she grimaced. 'Sorry. I was trying not to wake you.'

'You didn't. I heard Bea huffing and puffing so thought I'd heat up her bottle. That little madam really lets you know when she's hungry!'

'In training to be a proper little princess,' Polly said, laughing.

'Too right. Anyway, where are you off to? I take it that call was from one of your mums?'

'Amy Carmichael.' Polly quickly explained the situation to her.

Beth sighed. 'Poor Amy. I feel for her. It must be a lot to deal with.'

'It must.' Polly sighed. 'It brings it home to me just how awful it must have been for Elliot when Joseph was born.'

'He has spina bifida, doesn't he?' Beth said. 'One of the mums I met at the clinic the other day mentioned it. Her son's in the same class at school as Joseph, apparently.'

'That's right, although he doesn't let it slow him down, believe me. He's a great little boy, full of fun and interested in everything.'

'You're fond of him then?'

'Oh, yes. It would be hard not to be. He's so plucky.'

'So you're fond of the child and have fallen for the father,' Beth declared, her eyes twinkling. 'Do I need to buy myself a new hat?'

'No!' Polly rolled her eyes. 'You've still got the one you bought for my *last* wedding—the wedding that was called off. No way am I going down that particular road again in a hurry!'

'If you say so. Anyway, give Amy my love, won't you?'

Beth disappeared into the kitchen, leaving Polly to let herself out. However, as she got into her car, she couldn't help thinking about what Beth had said. Even though there was no chance of it happening, she found herself wondering how it would feel to walk down the aisle and see Elliot waiting for her...

She drove the thought from her mind as she started the engine. It was pointless wasting time thinking about something that was never going to happen!

Elliot was eating his breakfast when he received a text message from the hospital informing him that Amy Carmichael was on her way in. Leaving the rest of his toast, he hurried upstairs to fetch his jacket. Fortunately, Mrs Danton had arrived early so he didn't need to worry about Joseph. He ran back downstairs and quickly kissed his son then left. It was a beautiful day, a clear blue sky proclaiming that spring had arrived at last. The weather hadn't been this good since the day he had taken Joseph to the waterfall, he thought, then sighed when it immediately unleashed a host of memories he would have preferred not think about. He needed to concentrate on this baby and not start thinking about Polly again.

It was still early and traffic was light so he made good time. He went straight to the maternity unit, where he found a team of doctors waiting. Amy was coming in by ambulance and she hadn't arrived yet so he drew his colleagues aside and ran through the procedure they would need to follow when the baby was born. His opposite number from Obstetrics, Melanie Price, was also briefing her team. This baby would need all their expertise if he was to survive.

The ambulance arrived at last and the paramedics rushed Amy into the unit. Elliot felt his heart jolt when he realised that Polly was with them. She was talking to Amy and didn't appear to have noticed him. She suddenly looked up and he saw the colour run up her cheeks when she spotted him standing on the far side of the room. Just for a moment their eyes met before she looked away, but it was enough to tell him that she was remembering everything that had happened the other night. Heat poured through his veins. Polly might have had her reasons for halting that kiss but it didn't mean she hadn't wanted it. And him.

\* \* \*

Polly could feel Elliot's eyes on her as she helped Amy move onto the bed. She should have realised he would be here, she thought as she made Amy comfortable. Elliot and his team would be responsible for the baby after he was born and they needed to be on hand, but she hadn't given any thought to the fact that she would see him. It was hard to focus on what needed to be done when she was conscious of his gaze following her every move.

'You won't leave me, will you, Polly?' Amy pleaded, gripping tight hold of her hand. 'Rob's on his way home but he won't get here until tonight. I don't think I can do this on my own.'

'You won't be on your own, love. There's a whole team of doctors and midwives here to help you,' Polly explained, but it had little effect. She winced when Amy's grip on her hand tightened.

'I don't want them—I want you!' Amy declared.

Polly sighed when she heard the growing hysteria in Amy's voice. Amy needed to stay calm if she was to follow their instructions and she wouldn't be able to do that if she started to panic. Although it wasn't normal procedure for her to stay and help with a birth in the hospital, she knew it would be better for Amy.

'I can't see that it will present a problem if Sister Davies stays to help, can you, Ms Price?'

Polly looked up when Elliot spoke, surprised that he, of all people, should support her. Bearing in mind his views on community midwives, it was the last thing she would have expected.

'I'm sure it isn't necessary,' Melanie Price replied stiffly. 'My staff are all highly skilled when it comes to a difficult birth like this one.'

'I'm sure they are. However, I doubt if they're better qualified than Sister Davies. I have been lucky enough to work with her before and I can assure you that you won't find anyone more skilful than her.'

Elliot's tone was level but Polly heard the determination it held. She wasn't surprised when Ms Price reluctantly agreed that she could stay. She moved aside while one of the other midwives set up the monitoring equipment. The baby's blood pressure and heartbeat would be constantly checked so that they could tell if a problem arose during the delivery. A birth like this was far from straightforward and they needed all their resources if the baby was to survive. Amy was having regular contractions now so, once the equipment was in place, Polly moved back to the bed and quietly reminded her about everything she had learned in the antenatal classes she had attended. The calmer Amy was, the easier it would be for her and the baby.

It was a couple more hours before the baby was born, by which time Amy was exhausted, both by the physical strain of her labour and the emotional trauma. She could barely raise her head to look at her son before he was whizzed away by one of the neonatal team.

'What happens now?' she whispered.

'Dr Grey and his team are intubating him and starting ventilation,' Polly explained, glancing over to where Elliot was working to stabilise the little boy. He looked up and nodded and she breathed a sigh of relief because it appeared that the first step had been successful. She smiled at Amy. 'They've done that so they will take him to the neonatal unit now.'

'And then what's going to happen?' Amy asked, tears starting to trickle down her face.

'He'll be closely monitored and once it's clear that his lungs are strong enough then the hole in his diaphragm will be repaired.'

'And he'll be all right after that?' Amy said hopefully. 'Once he's had the operation, he'll be fine?'

'He may need support with his breathing for several weeks afterwards,' Polly warned her because it would be wrong to let Amy think that everything was cut and dried. She needed to prepare herself for the fact that her baby would need a lot of extra care in the early days. 'He will probably need help with feeding as well but the nurses on NICU will show you what to do, so there's no need to worry about that.'

'And you'll be there when I take him home if I have any problems,' Amy said, sounding relieved.

Polly didn't say anything but just smiled. She didn't want to upset Amy any more by explaining that she would be leaving Beesdale very shortly. She helped one of the other midwives to deliver the placenta but the thought preyed on her mind. It was upsetting to know that she wouldn't be able to play any part in this baby's life in the future. Once she left then Amy and the rest of her mums would become the responsibility of someone else and she hated to think that she would no longer be involved in their care.

Was she making the right decision? she wondered then sighed. She was no longer sure, if she was honest. She would be leaving so much behind, not just her mums and the town she loved, but Elliot as well. The thought of never seeing him again was incredibly painful, especially after the way he had spoken up for her earlier. If she stayed, was there a chance that he might come to care for her? It was a tantalising thought even though she knew that it was unlikely to happen. Elliot was still in love with his ex-wife and he still bore the scars from her leaving him. There was no place for Polly in his life or in his heart.

Elliot was quietly optimistic when he left NICU a short time later. The hole in baby Carmichael's diaphragm was less than an inch long, which meant that only a small section of his gut had entered his chest cavity.

Although Elliot had ordered an ultrasound to be done on the baby's heart, as CDH could be associated with other abnormalities, he didn't think that was the case in this instance. The baby was responding well to initial treatment, although it was too early to say if he would survive. It depended on how much lung tissue had been damaged but Elliot was hopeful that he would pull through. He hated to think how upset Polly would be if the baby died.

He sighed as he made his way to the coffee shop in the foyer. Once again he was relating everything that happened to Polly. He knew he should stop but it was hard. She gave so much of herself to the mums she cared for and it had brought it home to him once more how wrong he had been about her and the job she did. There was a place for community midwives and it was Polly who had made him understand that—Polly who had changed his view about so many things. He was a different person since he had met her.

Rounding the corner, Elliot stopped dead when he came face to face with the person who seemed to constantly occupy his thoughts. Polly ground to a halt as well, her face colouring, and he frowned. Was she thinking about the other night and feeling guilty? Wishing it had never happened? Logic shouted a resounding *yes* but he wasn't listening to logic at that moment. He was listening to his heart and it was screaming, *no, no, no!* So, if it was right, why had Polly stopped him kissing her, stopped *herself* from kissing him back? All of a sudden Elliot knew that he wouldn't rest until he found out the real answer.

'Hi! I was hoping you hadn't left,' he said quickly. 'I wanted to fill you in on how Amy's baby is doing.' He nodded towards the coffee shop in the corner of the foyer. 'I could murder a cup of coffee—how about you?'

'Oh…erm…well, all right then.'

Elliot hurriedly led the way when he heard the hesitation in her voice, not wanting to give her time to reconsider. The place was busy as usual but he spotted an empty table near the window and pointed to it. 'If you grab that table, I'll fetch the coffee. What do you want?'

'Just a filter coffee,' she told him, and he nodded.

'Okey-dokey. Won't be long.'

Elliot joined the queue, trying to contain

his impatience as he waited his turn. Now that he had decided on a course of action, he was eager to get on with it. He ordered two filter coffees and two bacon rolls to go with them and paid at the till. Polly was staring out of the window when he went back to the table and he found himself admiring the purity of her profile before he forced himself not to get side-tracked. He needed a clear head if he was to solve this mystery and he couldn't achieve that if he was thinking about how much he wanted her. The thought made his hands tremble and he grimaced when coffee slopped over the sides of the cups as he set the tray on the table.

'Sorry. I'll fetch some more napkins to wipe that up.'

'Don't bother—it's fine.'

Polly took one of the cups off the tray. Running her finger down the side, she mopped up the coffee. Elliot's head began to pound when he saw her lift her finger to her mouth and lick it. There was something incredibly erotic about the gesture...

'I got us a couple of bacon rolls as well,' he said, desperate to ward off the thoughts that were rioting around his head. Thinking about how her tongue would taste, flavoured with coffee, was never going to help him focus! 'I didn't know if you preferred brown sauce or red so I got both.'

He dumped a handful of sauce packets onto the table and sat down, praying that she couldn't tell how keyed up he felt. What was it about Polly that made him feel this way? He had made up his mind a long time ago that he would never get involved with a woman again and yet Polly only had to do something as innocuous as lick her finger and he forgot about all that. All he could think about was how wonderful it would be to hold her in his arms and know that she would be his for ever. Was he falling in love with her? His heart lurched. He must be if he was willing to risk being hurt again.

Polly could feel the tension in the air and wished with all her heart that she had refused the offer of coffee. No good would come of spending more time with Elliot, would it? It merely reminded her how much she was going to miss him when she left. Picking up the cup, she took a sip of the coffee, hoping it would steady her. Elliot was speaking and she forced herself to concentrate. The last thing she wanted was for him to guess how difficult this was for her. She had never been someone who hid her emotions but she had to hide them now.

'There's a long way to go before we can even consider the idea that the baby will make it, but I'm hopeful, shall we say.' He picked up a packet of sauce and squeezed some onto his bacon roll.

'Not many babies with CDH survive,' Polly said carefully, measuring every word.

'Sadly, not.' He sighed as he wiped his fingers on a paper napkin. 'Over eighty per cent of babies diagnosed with CDH antenatally die either before or straight after birth.'

'I didn't realise it was so many!' Polly exclaimed in genuine surprise.

'Unfortunately, yes. As you know, the condition is often linked to other abnormalities as well. However, if there aren't any then roughly half of those babies survive.'

'Do you think Amy's baby has anything else wrong with him?' she asked quickly, because it was better if she focused on something other than her own feelings.

'No. I've ordered an ultrasound of his heart

but I don't think there's anything else lurking in the background. If I'm right then he has a fifty-fifty chance of pulling through, assuming he survives the operation, of course.'

'Does Amy know all this?' Polly asked, her heart aching at the thought of Amy being hit with all this information. It was such a lot to take in.

'Not yet. I thought I'd wait until her husband gets home before I explain it all to them.' He shrugged. 'It might make it that bit easier for her if he's with her.'

Polly felt a wave of warmth invade her. Had Elliot's attitude softened because he could relate to how Amy was feeling? She knew it was true and her heart swelled with joy. That Elliot was allowing himself to actually feel some kind of emotion seemed like a giant step forward. It made her wonder what other steps he might be ready to take.

'I think that's a good idea,' she said, trying to damp down the excitement that filled her. Just because he had come this far, it didn't mean that he had undergone a complete change of heart. His feelings for his ex-wife must be extremely strong if he still loved her after what she had done. The thought sent a

shaft of pain through her so that it was hard
not to show how she felt when he looked at
her.

'I'm glad you agree.' He suddenly smiled.
'It's good to know that I've done the right
thing for once.'

'Oh, you have!' Polly exclaimed. Impul-
sively, she reached across the table and laid
her hand on his. 'Amy needs her husband
with her at a time like this—they need each
other if they're to get through it.'

'That's what I thought,' he said huskily.
He turned his hand over and Polly's heart
lurched when she felt the warm strength of
his fingers enclosing hers. Her eyes rose to
his and her breath caught when she saw the
urgency they held. 'What you said the other
day, Polly—' He stopped abruptly when his
pager beeped. Letting go of her hand, he
checked the display. 'Maternity. A problem
with a baby whose heart rate is sky-high. I'll
have to go.' He stood up then paused. 'Joseph
keeps asking if you're still coming to tea on
Saturday. What should I tell him?'

'What do you want to tell him?' Polly
asked, holding her breath. She knew what she

wanted to do but it was up to Elliot to decide if he wanted it as well.

'That you're coming.'

'Then it's all decided.'

'So it is.' He gave her a slow smile before he turned away.

Polly watched until he disappeared into the lift. Only then did she let out the breath she'd been holding. Excitement was fizzing through her veins as she picked up the tray and took it over to the rack. She had no idea what was going to happen after Saturday but for now it was enough to know that Elliot wanted her in his life, even if it was only for a few hours.

# CHAPTER TWELVE

ELLIOT COULDN'T REMEMBER the last time he had felt so nervous. As he put the finishing touches to the table, he thought back over all the major events in his life. His final exams had passed without a flicker of nerves showing, as had his rotations, *despite* the fact that the first consultant he had worked for had been a tartar. His wedding day had been more a trial than anything else but even then he hadn't suffered from nerves. Joseph's birth had been incredibly stressful, but once again he hadn't felt nervous, merely determined to do his very best for his son. And yet here he was, all wound up, because Polly was coming for tea!

The doorbell rang and Elliot dropped the napkins he was holding on the floor. He stooped down to pick them up, hearing the sound of Joseph's wheelchair whizzing along

the hall as he went to let her in. Joseph was
thrilled that Polly was coming that evening
and it brought it home to Elliot all of a sudden
just how careful he needed to be. He didn't
want Joseph becoming attached to her just yet.

'Polly's here,' Joseph announced happily,
leading the way into the kitchen.

Elliot felt the butterflies in his stomach
multiply tenfold when he found Polly standing in front of him as he straightened up. He
had only ever seen her wearing jeans or her
uniform before but tonight she had chosen to
wear a dress and he couldn't drag his gaze
away from her. His eyes skimmed over her,
drinking in every detail, from how the deep
amber colour complimented the richness of
her red hair to the way the silky fabric clung
to every delicious curve. She looked beautiful—so beautiful that she completely stole his
breath. He could only stand there and stare at
her like some mindless idiot.

'I hope I'm not too early.' She hesitated
when Elliot didn't say anything then hurried
on. 'I don't think we actually set a time but if
it's awkward then I can come back later—'

'No!' The word exploded from his lips and
he saw her jump. He dredged up a smile but

he could feel himself cringing. *Idiot* was too kind a description for him. *Moron* would be more accurate! 'Of course you aren't too early. We're just pleased that you could come, aren't we, Joseph?' he said, passing the baton to his son in the hope that Joseph would make a better job of welcoming her than he was doing.

'Yes. It's brilliant,' Joseph declared enthusiastically. 'You'll be able to play a game with me while Dad finishes making the tea.'

'That sounds like fun, so long as your dad doesn't need any help.'

She looked at him and once again Elliot felt the words disappear down some long dark tunnel. Digging them out again was far too difficult so he simply shook his head. He felt relief wash over him when she gave him a quick smile then turned away. At least he had a breathing space now, time to get his act together. What was that expression Joseph used? Chillax—that was it. He needed to do exactly that, chill out and relax, or this evening was going to turn into a complete disaster.

Polly ate everything that was put in front of her, although she couldn't have named a single thing she had eaten afterwards. She kept thinking about the way Elliot had looked at her when she had arrived. A shiver ran down her spine as she recalled the expression in his eyes. He had looked at her the way a man looked at a woman he wanted, but was it true? Did he want her? And, if so, what was he going to do about it?

That question unleashed a maelstrom of feelings so that she found it difficult to follow the conversation. It was a relief when Elliot got up to make the coffee. Joseph asked if he could watch a DVD and headed to the television after he had helped to clear away his dishes. Polly collected up the glasses and took them to the sink. 'Shall I wash these?' she asked, glancing over to where Elliot was filling the coffee maker.

'No, it's fine. They can go in the dishwasher along with everything else.' He opened the dishwasher and started to load the dirty dishes into it, rolling his eyes when she handed him the glasses. 'Thank heavens for dishwashers. I don't mind doing most jobs but I absolutely hate washing dishes.'

'Some of us don't have any choice,' she replied tartly, and he laughed.

'Sorry! I didn't mean to touch a nerve, although you could always buy yourself a dishwasher if it would make life easier.'

'I'd need somewhere to put it and at the moment I don't even have that,' she told him wryly.

'Of course. What's happening about the cottage? Is the landlord sorting it out?'

'I'm not sure. I've spoken to the letting agents and they've been in touch with the owners but they're being very evasive, apparently,' she explained. 'They won't say when they're going to start the repairs. They've also refused to let me move into one of the other cottages in the meantime, so I don't know what's going on.'

'So where are you living at the moment?' Elliot asked and she was warmed to hear genuine concern in his voice.

'I'm staying with Beth, although it's a bit of a squeeze. She's one of the doctors at The Larches,' she added when he looked blank. 'She's on maternity leave at the moment, although she's planning to return to work later in the year. Her cottage is only small though, so fitting in an extra person now she has baby Beatrix isn't easy.'

'I see. What about the baby's father—is he not around?' he asked curiously.

'No.' Polly sighed. 'Beth and Callum split up before she discovered she was pregnant. She wrote and told Callum she was expecting his baby but he's not made any attempt to contact her, so she can only assume that he doesn't want anything to do with Beatrix.'

'Some people don't deserve to have children,' he said harshly, slamming the dishwasher door.

Polly sighed as he went back to the coffee maker. It was obvious that he was thinking about what Joseph's mother had done and it hurt to know that it still had such a huge effect on him. Would he ever get over it? she wondered sadly. Would he ever reach a point where he could let go of the past and concentrate on the future? She hoped so but, from what she had seen, it seemed unlikely. It was a depressing thought and she tried not to think about it as she found cups and saucers and loaded them onto a tray. Once the coffee was ready, Elliot put the carafe on the tray as well.

'Shall we have this in the sitting room?' He glanced over to where Joseph was engrossed in a film about dinosaurs, grimacing when a couple of the creatures started fighting. 'It should be a bit quieter in there, not to mention a lot less gory!'

'Surely you're not put off by a drop of blood, Doctor?' Polly taunted.

Elliot laughed as he picked up the tray. 'A drop is fine. What I don't fancy is watching buckets of the stuff swilling all over the place while I drink my coffee.'

Polly laughed as well as she hurried along the hall and opened the sitting room door, taking heart from the fact that he had responded to her teasing. Elliot had changed a lot from the uptight man he'd been when they had met, and who was to say that he wouldn't change even more? Drawing over the coffee table in front of the sofa, she waited while he placed the tray on it, trying to keep a rein on the excitement fizzing through her veins. She mustn't forget that she might not be around to witness the transformation if it did happen.

'Shall I pour?' she suggested, blanking out that thought because it was too painful.

'Please.' Elliot huffed out a sigh as he sat down. 'Phew, am I glad that's over. I'm not the world's best cook, as you probably could tell, but Joseph insisted that we should do the cooking ourselves tonight in honour of your visit. That's why we ended up with sausage and mash. I have a very limited repertoire, so I can only apologise if you were expecting something a tad more sophisticated.'

Polly laughed when he rolled his eyes. 'There's no need to apologise. I love sausage and mash, as it happens. I much prefer something like that to all those cheffy meals you see on the television.'

'You mean you don't go in for foam and micro herbs?' He shook his head in mock dismay. 'Heavens above, woman, have you no taste at all?'

'Not when it comes to folk using tweezers to primp my dinner,' she retorted, loving the fact that he was teasing her now. That he felt relaxed enough to do so set up a warm little glow inside her and she replied in the same joking vein. 'Don't tell me that's the sort of food you prefer—quenelles of this and dots of that?'

'Nope. I like my food to look the way it's supposed to and not be turned into a culinary work of art.'

'It seems we agree on something then,' she said, chuckling.

'Oh, I think there's a lot of things we agree on,' he said softly. 'And not just food.'

Polly bit her lip when she heard the undercurrent in his voice. Was Elliot admitting that he felt something for her? However, before she could even attempt to process that thought, the telephone rang. Polly picked up the pot as Elliot excused himself and went to answer it, her thoughts in turmoil. Did she really want to move away when there was a chance that Elliot might want her to stay around? It was only when she saw the grim expression on his face as he came back into the room that she pulled herself together. She was in danger of reading far too much into an off-the-cuff remark.

'Has something happened?' she asked anxiously.

'An accident just outside Hemsthwaite. A couple ran into the back of a lorry that was parked in a lane. The woman was eight months pregnant and the paramedics had to deliver the baby at the scene. It's badly injured and they need me to go in and see what I can do.' He ran his hand through his hair.

'Mrs Danton is away this weekend so I'll have to take Joseph with me.'

'I can mind him,' Polly said immediately.

'Would you?'

'Of course. I've booked the evening off so I can stay here rather than you having to drag him all the way to the hospital at this time of the night.'

'That would be great, if you're sure you don't mind,' he began.

'Of course I don't mind,' she said firmly, cutting him off. 'Just tell him what's happening and then you get off. It sounds as though it's extremely urgent.'

'Thank you.' Crossing the room, he took hold of her hands and pulled her to her feet. Polly's breath caught when she felt his lips brush her cheek. 'I really appreciate this, Polly.'

'It's fine. Honestly,' she murmured with some difficulty as her lungs seemed to have locked tight. 'I'm only too happy to help.'

'I know.' He ran his knuckles down her cheek in the lightest of caresses imaginable. 'You're that kind of a person, Polly—someone who helps others even when they don't deserve it. You're very special, as I've come to realise.'

He bent and kissed her again, only this time on the mouth, and she shuddered. He didn't say a word as he let her go but he didn't need to. They both knew that the kiss was merely the forerunner to a whole lot more.

Polly sank back down onto the sofa, listening to the sound of his footsteps as he went to tell Joseph what was happening. Was she ready for this—ready to start a relationship, because that was where they were heading? After all, it was only a matter of weeks since her wedding had been called off, so was it too soon? It had been such a stressful time too, so was she in danger of misinterpreting her feelings?

The answers came flooding back—no, no and *no*! Polly felt excitement bubble up and spill over. All of a sudden she knew that this was what she wanted more than anything. She wanted to be with Elliot and if there was a chance of that happening then she would grab it with both hands.

The baby was too badly injured to save. Elliot did everything he could but not even his skills could make a difference. He thanked his team and left Theatre, dreading the next few minutes when he would have to tell the parents their baby daughter had died. It was never easy to break such news and tonight it would be even harder because he couldn't disengage his emotions as he normally would do. Tonight he felt overwhelmed by emotion and it was all down to Polly. She had unlocked the final barrier, destroyed his last defence. To say that he felt scared would be an understatement but there was nothing he could do.

He drove home afterwards, taking his time as he negotiated the narrow roads. It was two in the morning when he arrived at The Old Smithy and the house was in darkness, apart from a single light in the sitting room. Elliot switched off the engine and sat in the car for a moment while he gathered his thoughts. He knew what was going to happen—it was inevitable. But he needed to be sure that it was the right thing to do, not just for him but for Polly too. She had already told him that she would have felt guilty if they had continued kissing and this would be so much more than that. He couldn't bear to think that she might torture herself with regrets afterwards. Then there was him. He had sworn that he would never make a commitment to anyone again and he wasn't sure if he was ready to do so even now. Did Polly understand that? Could she accept it? He had no idea. All he knew was that if he and Polly made love, everything would change for both of them.

Elliot's pulse was racing as he let himself in. Dropping his keys onto the hall table, he made his way to the sitting room. The door was ajar and he could see Polly lying curled up on the sofa. The lamplight cast a golden glow over her face and once again he was struck by her beauty. It wasn't just a lucky combination of features either, but her inner beauty that shone through. She was as beautiful inside as out and he couldn't begin to understand why it had taken him so long to see that.

His heart was full as he went over to the sofa and sat down beside her. 'Hello, sleepyhead,' he murmured, running his finger down her cheek. Would she be willing to accept what he could offer her or wouldn't it be enough? The thought of losing her was more than he could bear but he had to be honest with her. He cared too much about her to lie.

'Oh, you're back.' She sat up, stifling a yawn. 'How did it go?'

'The baby didn't make it,' he said, struggling to control the sadness that filled him.

'Oh, I'm so sorry! How awful for the poor parents.'

'They were dreadfully upset, as you'd expect,' he said, his voice catching.

'They must have been.' She put her arms around him and hugged him. 'You did your best, Elliot. Nobody can do more than that.'

Elliot felt his eyes well with tears. All of a sudden, he found himself thinking about all the other babies he had been unable to save. He had locked away his grief about them for so long but now it all came pouring out, a huge tide that overwhelmed him.

'It's all right. Let it all out and you'll feel much better, I promise you.'

Elliot felt himself start to relax when Polly drew him towards her. It was a long time since anyone had held him like this, as though they truly cared. He could hear her whispering to him, a soft murmur of words that made little sense in his emotionally charged state yet which, oddly, comforted him. When she ran her hand down his back, he sighed. Maybe he was hurting but Polly made him feel better; she always would.

The thought was too much, coming on top of everything else that had happened that night. Elliot drew back, staring into her eyes as he searched for proof that he wasn't making a fool of himself. He had thought that Marianna had cared about him but he'd been wrong—very wrong. Could he trust his judgement when it had let him down so badly once before?

Polly's eyes met his and he shuddered when he saw the light they held. Polly truly cared about him and the realisation unlocked the very last of his reservations. There wasn't a single doubt in his mind that it was what he wanted as he leant forward and kissed her, no fear at all that he was making a dreadful mistake. This was Polly and he could trust her with his heart, if she was willing.

Polly felt a rush of desire fill her when Elliot's mouth settled over hers. Even though she had known this could happen, it hadn't prepared her for the way it made her feel. Closing her eyes, she gave herself up to the magic of his kiss. His lips were hard and demanding at first, exacting a response she was only too willing to give. Then slowly his lips gentled, giving even more than they demanded. Polly kissed him back, kissed him with every scrap of emotion she felt; she kissed him with tenderness and with passion, with joy and with love because that was what she felt. They were both breathing hard when they broke apart, both aware that they had reached a milestone. Whatever they decided now would determine what happened in the future.

'I didn't plan this, Polly. It was the last thing I wanted to happen, if I'm honest.' His voice grated and she shivered. She could tell the effort it had cost him to admit that and her heart ached at what he must be going through.

'I know. It wasn't something I'd planned either but, now that it has, we need to decide where we go from here.' She took a quick breath, trying to contain her fear. If Elliot decided that he didn't want this to go any further then she had to respect that.

'We do.' He took her face between her hands so that she was forced to look at him. 'I care about you, Polly. More than just care, in fact. But I need you to understand that I shall never get married again. I can't offer you that kind of commitment.'

Polly felt a searing pain slice through her. Elliot might care about her but he still wasn't over what had happened in the past. He probably never would get over it. It would always be there, an unseen barrier between them. Could she cope with the thought that he would never completely trust her, that he would always be influenced by another woman's actions? That he would never love *her* that much?

'I understand.' She drew back, trembling as she stood up. She didn't want to do this but she couldn't take what he was offering when she knew in her heart that it wasn't enough. 'I wish it could have been different, Elliot, really I do. You and I could have had something very special, but not if you don't trust me.'

'Of course I trust you!' he replied hotly, jumping to his feet.

'No, you don't. Not really.' She smiled sadly. 'If you trusted me then you'd know that I would never let you down. You'd know it in here.' She touched her heart. 'And, sadly, that's never going to happen unless you put the past behind you.'

'What about you? Have you put past events behind you?'

'What do you mean?' Polly said uncertainly.

'You told me that you'd have felt guilty if you hadn't called a halt the other night, so can you honestly say that you no longer have feelings for your former fiancé?' He laughed harshly. 'I don't think so. *This* is probably no more than a rebound from that!'

It was so far removed from the truth that Polly didn't know whether to laugh or cry. In the end she did neither, just picked up her bag and left. Elliot didn't follow her out and she was glad. It had been hard enough to do what was right. Tears welled in her eyes as she got into her car and backed out of the drive. It had been so tempting to take what he was offering but she couldn't make another wrong decision, even if it was for the right reason. She might have fallen in love with Elliot but it wasn't enough. She had to know that he loved her too.

# CHAPTER THIRTEEN

THE NEXT COUPLE of weeks passed in a blur. Elliot went into work and looked after Joseph but it felt as though he was functioning on autopilot. He kept thinking about what Polly had said. Was he allowing one bad experience to dictate his life? He knew it was true and yet the fear of making another mistake was too strong, especially when it wouldn't impact only on him but Joseph as well. How could he risk his son's happiness for the sake of his own?

It seemed that Joseph sensed that all wasn't right because he started acting up, causing a disruption in class and even getting into a fight with one of the other boys. He was no better at home, ignoring Mrs Danton whenever she asked him to do anything. Elliot guessed that he was upset because Polly hadn't visited them again, but it was no excuse. After an appointment at the school to speak to his class teacher, Elliot sat him down and had a stern word with him about his behaviour, but it had little effect. He was at his wits' end when Mrs Danton informed him that she wasn't prepared to look after Joseph any longer unless his behaviour improved.

In the end, Elliot managed to appease her but it simply added to the strain he was under. Once again, he found himself wondering if he had made a mistake by moving to the Dales. Between what had happened with Polly and Joseph's behaviour, he was ready to throw in the towel. It was only the thought of the upheaval it would cause that stopped him. That and a foolish desire to be near Polly. Even though he knew that she was probably on the rebound after splitting up from her fiancé, he couldn't help hoping that the situation might change. He sighed because if it did he would have to make some major changes too and he wasn't sure if he could find the courage to do that. It seemed they had reached an impasse.

He was ready to go home one evening when the sister from the maternity unit phoned him. They had delivered a baby boy who was suffering from heart problems and Melanie

Price, the obstetric consultant, had asked if he would examine him. Elliot agreed at once and headed straight to the unit. The baby had been intubated and was receiving oxygen but his skin was tinged blue. His sats were all over the place and the prognosis wasn't good. What made it all the more difficult was the fact that his mother had received no antenatal care during her pregnancy. She was with a group of travellers and had only recently arrived in the area so they had no history to go on, no ultrasound scans, nothing at all.

Elliot conferred briefly with Melanie and they both agreed that a scan needed to be done immediately. While it was being carried out, Elliot phoned home and told Mrs Danton that he would be late getting back. If it was the baby's heart then it could take some time to sort things out. He hung up, trying not to think about how his housekeeper had received the news. It was obvious that he would have to do something about Joseph's behaviour soon or he would find himself without anyone to look after his son. Just for a moment an image of Polly sprang to mind before he blanked it out. He couldn't ask Polly to help him after what had happened.

* * *

It was gone five when Polly got back to Beesdale. She had been over to Cumbria for the
interview and her mind was still racing with
all the things she had been asked. The most
difficult question had been why she wanted
to leave her present post. She had decided
not to get too personal so she had simply explained that her circumstances had changed
and she had decided to relocate. It seemed to
cover a multitude of sins, from her cancelled
wedding to what had happened with her and
Elliot, although it didn't explain half of what
she was going through. While she had no regrets about the wedding, she did regret turning down what Elliot had been offering her.
Had she been a fool to take such a stance?
Should she have accepted and hoped that, in
time, he would come to love and trust her?
The questions seemed to be on a never-end-
ing cycle, spinning round and round inside
her head all the time.

She was still staying with Beth as there was
no sign of her cottage being repaired. She let
herself in and headed straight to the kitchen
to switch on the kettle. Beth had told her that
she was going to visit a friend in Leeds and
that she and Beatrix would probably stay

there overnight, so Polly had the place to herself. She made herself a cup of tea and took it
back to the sitting room, kicking off her shoes
as she curled up on the sofa. It was good to
have some time to herself. Maybe it would
help her get everything straight in her head.

Although it was extremely tempting to
change her mind about her and Elliot, she
mustn't do it. Their relationship might work
for a while, but it wouldn't work for ever and
that was what counted. She didn't want to be
with him for a few months or even for a few
years; she wanted to be with him for ever.
And that kind of commitment was beyond
him. If she was offered the job in Cumbria,
she would take it. Once she had put down
some roots there then she would be able to
build a new life for herself...

*Even though she would never spend that
life with Elliot?*

Despair washed over her but there was
no point trying to ignore the truth. Her life
would never be complete without the man she
loved to share it.

Elliot had reached a critical point in the operation. It had turned out that two of the
baby's heart valves were damaged and he was

in the process of fitting new ones. To do so, a machine would need to take over the work of the baby's heart. It was crucial that the timing was right and everyone was waiting for him to give the signal to go ahead. The last thing he needed was any distractions so he was not happy when Grace Adams, the theatre sister, informed him there was an urgent telephone call for him.

'Tell them to phone back,' he said curtly, not taking his eyes off the monitor screen that was displaying the baby's heartbeat, oxygen levels and blood pressure, all vital pieces of information.

'I'm sorry, sir, but the caller was very insistent.' Grace hesitated, obviously wary of the fallout that could follow from interrupting him. She rushed on. 'She said something about your son going missing.'

Elliot felt his stomach go into freefall. He had to make a concerted effort to hold himself together. 'Put her on the speaker phone,' he snapped.

Grace nodded to another nurse who was standing behind the glass viewing screen and a moment later Mrs Danton's voice could be heard. Elliot felt his stomach sink even more when he heard the panic in her voice. 'It's Joseph, Dr Grey. He's gone missing. He's supposed to stay at school for chess club on a Thursday but the head teacher has just rung to say there's no sign of him.'

'Have they checked everywhere?' he demanded. 'Maybe he's in the toilets or gone back to his classroom—'

'No, they've looked and there's no sign of him anywhere,' Mrs Danton said, cutting him off. 'I didn't know what to do, whether I should call the police, which is why I phoned you.'

'I want you to phone the police immediately and explain what's happened. Then speak to the head again and let her know what you've done. The police will need to speak to her and we don't want to waste time tracking her down if she's gone home.' Elliot felt as though his head was going to burst as he tried to think what else needed to be done but all he could think about was Joseph being out on his own... He blanked out the thought because he couldn't deal with it. 'I'll be home as soon as I can. In the meantime, I want you to stay there in case he comes back. Understand?'

Silence filled the room when the line went

dead. Elliot took a deep breath to steady himself. Although the only thing he wanted to do was to find Joseph, he couldn't leave. Not yet. This baby would die if the operation didn't go ahead and then there would be another family grieving. It was the starkest of choices: his son or someone else's son, yet he knew what he had to do, knew that he wouldn't be able to live with himself if the baby died because he had failed him.

In that moment, he realised that the transformation was complete. He could never go back to the way he had been and he didn't want to either. Maybe it *did* hurt to allow his emotions free rein but it was better than living in an emotional wasteland. Sadness, joy, happiness and grief all had their place. So had fear. And love. Could one counteract the other? he wondered as he gave the signal to start the machine. He hoped so. If love could conquer his fear then maybe he could have Polly back in his life. He needed her more than ever at this moment!

Polly was making herself a sandwich when she heard a knock on the front door. Wiping her hands on a tea towel, she went to answer it and was shocked to find Elliot standing outside. 'What are you doing here?' she exclaimed.

'Joseph's gone missing,' he said tersely.

'Missing?'

'Yes. He was supposed to stay behind at school for chess club but he didn't turn up and nobody seems to know where he's gone.' He dragged his hand through his hair and she could see that he was trembling. 'He's been acting strangely for a while and now this—'

'Come in,' Polly said as his voice broke. She led him into the sitting room and made him sit down. 'What do you mean by acting strangely? In which way?'

'He's been disruptive in class and even got into a fight with another boy. And when he's at home, he keeps ignoring Mrs Danton when she asks him to do anything.' His eyes were filled with fear when he looked at her. 'It's not like him, Polly. Oh, I know he can be difficult at times—all kids can, I expect. But he's never behaved like this before.'

'Something's obviously upset him. Do you have any idea what it might be?' she asked, her heart aching at the thought of what Joseph might be going through.

'No, none at all. He's been asking about you and when we'll see you again so it might be that, although it seems a bit extreme, doesn't it?'

'It does.' She bit her lip but the idea needed to be considered. 'You don't think he's heard those rumours, do you?'

'About us?' He shrugged. 'I doubt it. Anyway, it's far more likely that he'd be pleased at the thought of you and me rather than upset. He's very fond of you, Polly.'

'I'm very fond of him too,' she said, feeling a lump come to her throat.

'I know you are.' He covered her hand with his and she had the feeling that he wanted to say something more before he thought better of it. He stood up abruptly. 'I'd better go. I'm going to drive around and see if I can find him. He can't have gone that far.'

'I'll have a look as well,' she said immediately. 'I know the area better than you do so I can check any places you might miss.'

'Thank you. I appreciate it, especially after what's happened.' Capturing her hands, he drew her to him. 'I know this isn't the right time, but once this is over then we need to talk, Polly.'

'I'm not sure if we have anything to talk about,' she said, her voice catching.

'Oh, I think we do.' Bending, he kissed her softly on the mouth then left.

Polly put her fingers to her lips, shuddering when she felt the warmth of his mouth imprinted on hers. Maybe she was jumping to conclusions but there had been something in his voice that filled her with a sudden sense of hope. Was Elliot ready to put the past behind him at last? The idea was just too immense to deal with right then. She had something more pressing to worry about now, namely finding Joseph. However, once he was safely back home then she would think about it, not only think but ask questions too. She sighed. There was still a long way to go. She needed to be sure that Elliot was ready to make a lifetime's commitment. Nothing less would do.

By eight o'clock Elliot was frantic with worry. There was still no sign of Joseph. The police had interviewed his classmates but they had been unable to shed any light on his whereabouts either. In another hour it would be dark and the thought of his son being out on his own at night terrified the life out of him. Joseph had to be somewhere! He couldn't just disappear. It was finding him that was proving so difficult.

In the end, Elliot went home to check if Joseph had made his way back there. If he thought he was in trouble for going missing then he might have hidden in one of the outbuildings. Elliot checked the shed and the disused stables even though the police had already searched them. He also searched the garden, looking behind the bushes and calling Joseph's name, but there was no sign of him there. The police had taken away one of his sweaters as they were bringing in the sniffer dogs in the hope they might be able to track him down. They had also alerted the local search and rescue team and they were out on the hills, looking for him, although it was unlikely he could have got very far in his wheelchair.

Elliot knew that everything possible was being done but it still wasn't enough. He couldn't bear to imagine what his life would be like if they never found him. He loved him so much and if—*when!*—he got him home again he would tell him that, just as he intended to tell Polly how much he loved her.

One thing was certain after this: he was going to make sure the people he loved knew how he felt!

Polly scoured the town, checking all the nooks and crannies where a child might hide, but there was no sign of Joseph anywhere. She drew up outside the store and hurried inside to buy a bottle of water before she continued her search. It was a warm, dry evening and her only consolation was that at least Joseph wasn't out in bad weather. Maureen Bishop was serving behind the counter and she raised her eyes when she saw Polly come in.

'Are you looking for that little lad that's gone missing?' She carried on when Polly nodded. 'I thought you were, you being such a good friend of his father and all. He must have got lost on the way to your place. I gave him directions but it's a long way, especially in a wheelchair.'

'I'm sorry, but are you saying that you gave Joseph directions to Dr Andrews' house?' Polly queried.

'No, of course not!' Maureen said indignantly. 'I sent him to Primrose Cottage.

That's where you've been living since you and Martin split up, isn't it?'

Polly didn't wait to hear anything else as she raced out of the shop. Was it possible that Joseph had gone all the way to the cottage to look for her? She sped through the town, praying that she wouldn't meet any traffic on the way. It was getting dark when she drew up and she switched on the headlights, using the light from them to search the front garden as well as the lane. She could hear the river flowing past in the background and paused, remembering how Joseph had loved the sight of the water when they'd been at the waterfall that day. Was it possible that he had gone to look at the river?

She raced around the side of the cottage, her heart leaping into her throat when she saw his wheelchair on the riverbank. There was no sign of Joseph, however, and her fear intensified as she made her way to the edge of the bank and peered down into the water, gasping in dismay when she spotted him clinging hold of some bulrushes. The lower half of his body was in the water and it was clear that he hadn't been able to pull himself out.

Polly scrambled down the bank and waded in, shivering as the cold water rose to the level of her thighs. Wrapping her arm around Joseph's waist, she lifted him clear of the water. 'I'm going to help you back up the bank, sweetheart,' she explained, feeling him trembling with a combination of cold and fear. 'Try to grab hold of the plants, will you? It will make it easier.'

Joseph nodded, too exhausted to speak. Polly took a firmer grip on him, knowing that it was vital that she got him out of the water as quickly as possible. Even in the middle of summer the water temperature in British rivers was barely above freezing point and she knew how quickly hypothermia could set in. The thought seemed to give her added strength so that she was able to boost Joseph up until he reached the top of the bank. Once she was sure he wouldn't slip back down again, she hauled herself out. They were both soaking wet and covered in mud but it was Joseph she was concerned about. She needed to get him out of his wet clothes and into something dry.

She fetched the wheelchair over and helped him into it then hurried him back to her car.

She had an assortment of spare clothes in the boot so once she had stripped him and rubbed him dry, she dressed him in those. Pulling the hood of her raincoat over his head, she bent down beside him. 'Do you know how long you were in the water, sweetheart?'

'No, but it felt like ages.' Tears welled in his eyes and he started to cry. 'I thought nobody would find me.'

'It must have been very scary,' Polly said, hugging him tight. 'You've been very brave. Not many little boys could have held onto those bulrushes the way you did. Now, I'm going to take you home to your dad. He will be so pleased to see you.'

'He won't be cross, will he?' Joseph looked beseechingly at her.

'No, he'll just be glad to have you back home,' she assured him.

Opening the passenger door, she helped him into the car and fastened his seat belt. The wheelchair was much too heavy for her to lift so she left it outside the cottage for Elliot to collect later. It didn't take long to drive to The Old Smithy. Polly pulled into the drive and sounded the horn. Joseph had fallen asleep on the way, worn out by his adventures, and there was no way she could lift him out and carry him inside. Elliot appeared almost immediately, the worry on his face changing to relief when he saw his son. He came rushing over to her.

'Where did you find him?'

'Primrose Cottage. He must have gone there to find me, although I've not asked him why.' She got out of the car, grimacing when her shoes squelched. 'He'd fallen into the river and couldn't get out again so I had to go in after him. Fortunately, I had some dry clothes in the car and put them on him, but I don't know how long he was in the water so you'll have to keep an eye on him. He was very cold.'

'I don't know what to say.' Elliot shook his head. 'There aren't enough words to thank you, Polly. If you hadn't gone looking for him—' He broke off and shuddered.

'Don't think about it.' She touched his hand. 'Just concentrate on making sure Joseph is all right.'

'I will, but I shall be grateful to you for ever, Polly.' His eyes filled with tears all of a sudden. 'I don't know what I'd do if anything happened to him.' He paused then carried on and she couldn't fail to hear the conviction in his voice. 'I don't know what I'd do if anything happened to you, either.'

# CHAPTER FOURTEEN

POLLY PICKED UP a towel and started to rub herself dry. Elliot was in the bathroom with Joseph and she could hear the murmur of their voices coming along the landing. He had telephoned the police and informed them that Joseph had been found, safe and well. Although they would need to talk to Joseph to find out why he had gone missing, they had agreed to leave it until the following day. She had been going to drive straight back to Beth's house to shower and change but Elliot had insisted that she used the en suite bathroom attached to his bedroom. It was obvious that he wanted her there, although there was no guarantee that it meant anything, even after what he had said earlier. He probably felt beholden to her for finding Joseph.

Disappointment rippled through her but she tried her best to ignore it. Taking the bathrobe off the hook on the back of the door, she slipped it on. It was far too big for her but her clothes were in the washing machine and they wouldn't be ready for some time. She rolled up the sleeves and tied the belt tightly around her waist then made her way along the landing, smiling when she stopped outside the bathroom. It was good to see the two people who had come to mean so much to her laughing together.

'Looks like you two are having fun,' she said, going to join them.

'Oh, we are.' Elliot scooped up a handful of soap suds and deposited them on Joseph's head. 'What do you think of his new hairstyle, Polly? A definite improvement, wouldn't you say?'

'I would.' Polly laughed when Joseph promptly retaliated, placing a handful of bubbles on Elliot's chin. 'Hmm, I rather like the white beard. Very appropriate for your age, I have to say.'

'Careful, or you could end up with a few *improvements* of your own,' Elliot warned her, his eyes gleaming with laughter. 'What do you think, Joseph?'

'Yes!' Joseph grinned as he scooped up a

handful of suds. He formed them into a ball and threw them at Polly, laughing when she was showered with soap suds. 'You look as if you've been snowed on!'

'Oh, you'll be sorry you did that, young man!' Polly retorted, dipping her hand into the foam. Elliot joined in as well so that very soon the bathroom was covered in soap suds.

'Right, I think it's time you came out of there, Joseph, before you turn into a prune,' Elliot declared, pulling out the plug. He wrapped Joseph in a towel and picked him up.

'I'll clear up in here while you dry him,' Polly offered.

'Thanks. That will save me a job.'

Polly felt her heart lift when he smiled at her. Maybe she was in danger of reading more into it than it actually meant, but she didn't think so. The thought stayed with her as she mopped up the mess. It took a while before everywhere was set to rights again and, by the time she had finished, Joseph was in bed. She went over and kissed him, feeling a lump come to her throat when he wound his arms around her neck and hugged her.

'I love you, Polly,' he declared.

'And I love you too, sweetheart,' she replied, praying that she wasn't doing the wrong thing by saying that. After all, there was no guarantee that Elliot wanted her to play any part in Joseph's life, was there?

'And you don't mind if my legs don't work like other boys' and girls' legs do?'

'Of course not!' Polly exclaimed. 'I think you are a very special little boy. No wonder your daddy is so proud of you. I am too.'

'George said that you wouldn't want me 'cos of my legs,' Joseph told her guilelessly. 'He heard his mummy talking and she said that she wouldn't want a child who couldn't walk and that you wouldn't want me either.'

'That isn't true,' Polly said firmly. She glanced at Elliot and went cold when she saw the expression on his face. It was obvious that he had retreated into himself again and she couldn't help wondering if it might be permanent. She forced the thought aside because she needed to make sure that Joseph understood how wrong he was. 'It doesn't matter if your legs don't work, sweetheart. You are still the bravest little boy I have ever met and I'd be very proud if you were mine.'

She kissed him again, aware that she had overstepped the mark by miles by saying that. Her heart was racing as she made her way downstairs while Elliot tucked Joseph up. Every word she'd said was true, but how would Elliot feel about it?

Elliot felt as though his head was about to burst. Had Polly meant what she'd said? Was she really willing to take on the responsibility of a child with a handicap like Joseph's? It was a huge commitment for any woman and Polly wasn't just any woman—she was the woman he loved. He longed for it to be true but he was afraid to let himself hope that it was. He knew that if Polly hadn't meant it then it would be the end for them. He couldn't and wouldn't risk Joseph's heart being broken by being let down again.

Polly was standing by the fireplace when Elliot went into the sitting room. Her head was bowed and the expression on her face made his stomach churn. It was obvious that she was having second thoughts and he knew what about too. Oh, maybe she had meant to be kind, but she should never have told Joseph that and led him to think that she wanted to be part of his life. Elliot felt a rush of anger seize him. She should never have led *him* to believe that she wanted to be part of *his* life either!

'I hope you're pleased with yourself,' he snapped, trying to contain the agony he felt. Somewhere along the line he had started to dream about the future and it had been a huge mistake.

'I beg your pardon?' She turned to face him and he felt himself waver when he saw the pain in her eyes. However, he couldn't afford to worry about her feelings when it was Joseph who mattered.

'What you told Joseph just now was completely out of order. How dare you let him think that you really care?'

'How dare I?' She rounded on him in fury. 'How dare you, you mean. I told him the truth and if you don't like it then there's not a lot I can do. It's not my fault if you've got a massive hang-up about women, Elliot. It isn't my fault either that Joseph's mother ran out on you. I'm sorrier than I can say that your ex-wife hurt you, Elliot, but you must know by now that I am nothing like her!'

'No. You're not.' Elliot felt a huge great wave of relief wash over him. All of a sudden all those doubts he'd had seemed pitiful.

Polly was right because he *had* allowed past events to influence his thinking. He took a step towards her, seeing the wariness on her face and he understood why. They'd had their differences ever since they had met, but now it was time they faced up to how they really felt. He smiled to himself. Polly was as guilty as him in her own way. She too had tried to hide her real feelings, but that was about to change if he had anything to do with it.

'You're not like any woman I've ever met.' He touched her cheek, his breath catching when he felt the softness of her skin. It took a massive effort of will not to let himself be side-tracked. 'You're brave and strong and loving and caring and I adore you, even though it's giving me hot and cold chills to admit. I'm sorry I said what I did just now. I was scared because I can't bear the thought of Joseph getting hurt.'

'I would never hurt him.' She looked into his eyes and he shuddered when he saw the conviction in her gaze. 'I would never hurt you either, Elliot. I love you both far too much to risk hurting you.'

'Oh, Polly!'

The rest of what he'd been about to say

got swept away as she stepped into his arms. Elliot held her close, held her as though he would never let her go again. He couldn't remember feeling like this before, safe and completely secure, and it overwhelmed him. He bent and kissed her, letting his lips say everything he couldn't put into words. He'd had so little practice at expressing his feelings but it didn't seem to matter: Polly understood everything he was trying to say. There were tears on both their faces when they broke apart but they were tears of joy and relief and he wasn't ashamed of them. He wanted her to know how deeply he felt about her, about them, about their future together.

'I love you, my darling, and I want us to be together for ever if it's what you want,' he whispered, holding her close so that he could feel her heart beating in time with his.

'It is.' She kissed him gently on the mouth then sighed. 'Oh, I know some folk will think it's far too soon to be starting another relationship, but this is what I want. I've never felt like this about anyone before.'

'Not even your fiancé?' he asked, because he had to know.

'No.' She took his hand and led him to the

sofa, nestling her head on his shoulder when they sat down. 'My feelings for Martin were based on what happened in the past. My parents died when I was twelve, you see, and my brother and I went to live with Martin and his parents. It was a huge upheaval, not only losing my parents but leaving everything I knew. I think that was the reason I agreed to marry him. He represented security and familiarity, and they were things I was desperate to hold on to. However, I was never really in love with him.'

'So you aren't pining to get back with him?' Elliot said, his head spinning.

'No.' She laughed softly. 'When I told you that I felt guilty it was because I was afraid that *you* would regret it if we'd carried on kissing. It had nothing to do with Martin.'

'How could I have got it so wrong?' He shook his head. 'I thought you were still in love with him and that you were on the rebound.'

'I know. But you were completely wrong. I care about Martin as a friend but I'm not in love with him—I never was. I know that now.'

'Because you love me?' he said, holding his breath.

'Yes.' She kissed him gently then drew back and he could see the sudden fear in her eyes. 'You said just now that you love me, but do you? Really? It wasn't just gratitude that made you say that because I'd found Joseph?'

'No. You can put that idea right out of your head.' He kissed her lingeringly and would have loved to carry on kissing her, only they needed to get everything straight before they went any further. The thought of what 'further' might entail made his heart race and he hurried on. 'I love you, Polly, and it's not just because you brought Joseph back home, although that's part of it in a way.' He took her face between his hands so that there would be no doubt about what he was saying. 'It's typical that you would risk your life to rescue him from the river. It's part and parcel of who you are, another reason why I fell in love with you. You're not only beautiful but you're brave and kind and...'

'Stop! I'll get a swelled head if you carry on showering me with compliments,' she protested, and he laughed.

'No way. It's not in your nature. I'm just trying to make sure you understand that I love everything about you. It's what makes you so special.'

'And what about Joseph's mother? Are you really over her?'

'I was over her a long time ago. Any feelings I'd had for her quickly died after we were married.' He sighed. 'I was ready to ask her for a divorce when she discovered she was pregnant. That's why we stayed together—for the sake of the baby.'

'I see. It must have been difficult.'

'As I told you, it was, especially when we found out that Joseph had spina bifida. I only wish I'd kept a closer eye on her from the start of the pregnancy.'

'What do you mean?' Polly asked, frowning.

'Marianna was very vain. I had no idea that she wasn't taking the folic acid supplement her consultant had prescribed for her. She'd got some crazy idea into her head that it was causing her to put on extra weight—complete rubbish that she'd read online. I've always wondered if Joseph would have been born with his disability if I'd kept track of what she was doing.' He sighed. 'I've always felt guilty about it.'

'There was no way you could have forced her to take the supplement,' Polly protested. 'And no guarantee it would have changed anything either.'

'Do you really believe that?'

'Yes, I do. Joseph is Joseph and he's a brilliant little boy, so be proud of him.'

'Oh, I am!' He hugged her, loving the fact that she had made him feel so much better with just a few words of reassurance. 'Anyway, what happened with Marianna obviously had a big influence on my life. I swore I wouldn't get involved with anyone again, not when it could mean risking Joseph's happiness as well.'

'So it wasn't because you were still in love with his mother? I saw that photo in your study…' She broke off and he grimaced.

'That's there purely so Joseph could see what his mother looked like, no other reason. Even though she doesn't play any role in his life, I think it's important that he knows who she is.' He pulled her into his arms. 'There's only one woman I love, even though she has led me a merry dance these past few weeks.'

'Hmm, I think I prefer it when you're showering me with compliments,' she murmured then stopped when his mouth found hers. She sighed in contentment when he raised his head. 'Looks like I might not be leaving after all.'

'Leaving?' he echoed. 'Leaving Beesdale, do you mean?'

'Uh-huh. I had an interview today, as it happens. In Cumbria. They seemed quite keen.'

'You're not going to take it, are you?' he demanded.

'That depends.'

'On what?'

'You.' She looked into his eyes and smiled. 'Do you want to show me how much you want me to stay, Elliot?'

'More than anything!'

*Three months later...*

'It should be me leaving, not you.'

'No, it shouldn't. Stop worrying, I'll be fine at Beth's.'

Reaching up, Polly kissed him on the mouth, feeling excitement coursing through her. In just over twelve hours' time she and Elliot were getting married. His proposal had come out of the blue but she'd had no hesitation about accepting it. The past three months while they had been living together had proved that their relationship was going to last and now it was time to show everyone else that it would last too.

'Have I told you how much I love you?' he murmured, pulling her into his arms and kissing the tip of her nose.

'Hmm, I'm not sure.' She pretended to think then laughed when he picked her up and spun her round. 'OK, OK! You did happen to mention it, as I recall.'

'Too right I did, Miss Davies,' he growled. He kissed her again then drew back and stared at her. 'I hope you're going to pay a lot more attention when you're Mrs Grey.'

'I'll try, although I can't promise anything, you understand.' She smiled up at him, marvelling at the transformation that had taken place over the last few months. Elliot was no longer afraid to show his feelings, telling her how much he loved her at each and every opportunity. The fact that he felt so comfortable doing so proved he was completely over what had happened in the past. He trusted her and knew she would never let him down. He was her whole world, him and Joseph, although there would be a small but significant change to their circumstances in the not too distant future. All of a sudden Polly knew that she couldn't keep it a secret any longer. She wanted to share it with him so that when they stood before the altar tomorrow they would both know what they had to look forward to.

'You know I was feeling sick the other day,' she began.

'After you'd eaten that prawn sandwich,' Elliot interjected.

'Yes. Only I don't think it was the sandwich, after all.'

'No? So what was it?'

'I'll give you a clue.' She dipped her hand into her pocket and handed him what looked like a plastic stick. Elliot stared at it for a moment before his head lifted and she saw the shock on his face.

'You don't mean that you're…?'

'Yes! Congratulations, darling. You're going to be a father again!'

'I don't know what to say,' he began then stopped and swept her into his arms. 'This is the best news ever!'

'So you're pleased then?' she teased him because it was blatantly obvious how he felt.

'Pleased, delighted, thrilled—every one of those and more.' He kissed her hungrily and his face was alight with happiness when he drew back. 'You've given me so much, my love, and now this. I couldn't be happier.'

'Neither could I,' she whispered. She drew back and frowned. 'I hope Joseph is pleased when he finds out.'

'Of course he will be.' Elliot grinned. 'He's been dropping hints about how much fun it would be to have a little brother or sister.'

'Really? He's never said anything to me.'

'That's because I told him not to.' Elliot chuckled. 'I didn't want to scare you away by thinking you had to fulfil his request. I know how much you love him.'

'I do. Just as I'm going to love this new little addition to our family.' She kissed him softly then stepped back. 'Now, it's time I left. I'll see you and Joseph tomorrow in church. He is going to make a brilliant best man.'

'He is. He's so excited about it too. Just like me, in fact. I can't wait to put my ring on your finger and know that you're mine for ever and always.'

'Neither can I.' She smiled, loving him with every fibre of her being. 'One thing's certain. This wedding is definitely going to take place!'

* * * * *

*If you enjoyed this story, check out these other great reads from Jennifer Taylor*

**THE BOSS WHO STOLE HER HEART**
**REAWAKENED BY THE SURGEON'S TOUCH**
**THE GREEK DOCTOR'S SECRET SON**
**MIRACLE UNDER THE MISTLETOE**

*All available now!*